MY LAST DUCHESS

MY LAST DUCHESS

A NOVEL

by

IAIN CRICHTON SMITH

LONDON
VICTOR GOLLANCZ LIMITED
1971

ISBN 0 575 00702 8

PRINTED IN GREAT BRITAIN
BY EBENEZER BAYLIS & SON LIMITED
THE TRINITY PRESS, WORCESTER, AND LONDON

MY LAST DUCHESS

That's my last Duchess painted on the wall,
Looking as if she were alive. I call
That piece a wonder, now: Frà Pandolf's hands
Worked busily a day, and there she stands.
Will't please you sit and look at her? I said
'Frà Pandolf' by design, for never read
Strangers like you that pictured countenance,
The depth and passion of its earnest glance,
But to myself they turned (since none puts by
The curtain I have drawn for you, but I)
And seemed as they would ask me, if they durst,
How such a glance came there; so, not the first
Are you to turn and ask thus. Sir, 'twas not
Her husband's presence only, called that spot
Of joy into the Duchess' cheek: perhaps
Frà Pandolf chanced to say 'Her mantle laps
Over my lady's wrist too much,' or 'Paint
Must never hope to reproduce the faint
Half-flush that dies along her throat:' such stuff
Was courtesy, she thought, and cause enough
For calling up that spot of joy. She had
A heart—how shall I say?—too soon made glad,
Too easily impressed; she liked whate'er
She looked on, and her looks went everywhere.
Sir, 'twas all one! My favour at her breast,
The dropping of the daylight in the West,
The bough of cherries some officious fool
Broke in the orchard for her, the white mule
She rode with round the terrace—all and each
Would draw from her alike the approving speech,
Or blush, at least. She thanked men,—good! but thanked
Somehow—I know not how—as if she ranked

My gift of a nine-hundred-years-old name
With anybody's gift. Who'd stoop to blame
This sort of trifling? Even had you skill
In speech—(which I have not)—to make your will
Quite clear to such an one, and say, 'Just this
Or that in you disgusts me; here you miss,
Or there exceed the mark'—and if she let
Herself be lessoned so, nor plainly set
Her wits to yours, forsooth, and made excuse,
—E'en then would be some stooping; and I choose
Never to stoop. Oh sir, she smiled, no doubt,
Whene'er I passed her; but who passed without
Much the same smile? This grew; I gave commands;
Then all smiles stopped together. There she stands
As if alive. Will't please you rise? We'll meet
The company below, then. I repeat,
The Count your master's known munificence
Is ample warrant that no just pretence
Of mine for dowry will be disallowed;
Though his fair daughter's self, as I avowed
At starting, is my object. Nay, we'll go
Together down, sir. Notice Neptune, through,
Taming a sea-horse, thought a rarity,
Which Claus of Innsbruck cast in bronze for me!

ROBERT BROWNING

Part one

1

He knocked on the door of the small house, which, slanted
and as if squashed like plasticine, reminded him of a painting
he had once received by post from an Arts Club. It was called
"Church at Auvers" and showed under a marine sky a church
with squashed roof and squashed windows and, all in all, looked
like the sort of thunderstruck place where a witch might
worship. Along one of the yellow patches in the foreground
a woman was walking as if into a high wind; the whole
painting was eerie and odd, the product of Van Gogh's queer
imagination.

He knocked on the small door (the house did not collapse)
and a small dog leaping up at him did not subside till a large
bony red-cheeked woman came to the door and said:
"What is it you want?"
And, indeed, unshaven, wearing three jerseys one on top of
each other because he could not stop shivering, and with
shoes which were scuffed and lacking even the memory of
polish because he had been walking so long, and his thick
brown coat the pockets of which were filled with a miscellany
of trash—including a bunch of keys, a ring, a bottle of aspirins,
a Penguin book picked up but unread, and a shaving bag—
and also weighed down by the coins which had dropped
through a hole right to the very bottom lining, he must to
others look odd, and especially to this woman who looked like
a tough Saxon peasant, her face ridged and red, her eyes hard,
her coarse dress practically reaching her ankles.
"I wish to see Mr. Frith, the novelist," he said.
He said it as if he were the only novelist, as indeed to him
he was, the one to whom in his incredible pain he might come,
to sit at his feet and listen, the one who had written that
moving short novel which was said to be based on the death
of his first wife, where even a chair or a brooch glowed with

MLD–A*   9

the incandescence of terrible disaster and guilt, leaping up and striking at him as if it were a snake out of a hallway with its flat narrow head. It was to him he was pilgrimaging (Frith had of course gone on to write thicker and thicker and more convoluted books lacking however that radiance as of streets seen in youth which seem to lead straight into the recesses of the heart): and for whom else would he have taken that long journey by bus, winding its tedious way over hills and beside walls till, eventually given directions by a bucolic peasant leaning on a fence and smoking a pipe which emitted sparks in the cold wind, he had arrived. To whom else would he, like a ghost, naked as an egg, have made his blind way?

"What do you want to see him about?" She stood there guarding the inmate, a dragon at the door, a wedge against which like an insurance man he must push. Trying to control his pain and rage he said as reasonably as he could:

"I am an admirer. I wish to talk to him if I may. I have come a long distance. I want him to help me. I have come a long way and I should like to get back to the town tonight."

She gazed at him, he thought, with jealousy and disgust as if, day after day, she was allowing into her house people like him, failures, those who could not cope with the lightning strokes that levelled them to the brown earth, as if she had hoped instead to invite a man in a shining green car who would tell his chauffeur to wait while he handed in the coveted ribbon or star, the very latest in ribands or coronets. She must, he thought, be the third wife. She didn't answer him but opened the door and let him through. Then, as if washing her hands of him, she disappeared and left him standing at an open door from which he could see Frith himself standing as if in a cage, looking out of the window, his bald head smooth and white as an egg, his lilac bow-tie neatly tied, his green jacket beautifully pressed, his white hands resting delicately on the window sill, as if he might take off into the distances into which he was gazing.

He found himself at length (after some mute counterchangings) sitting in a chair opposite Frith who was chewing an apple which he had removed from a dish on the table, behind him row after row of books, magazines, pamphlets, in different languages, Italian, French, Greek and German. Frith drew his chair closer to the fire as if he were cold and he himself adjusted the blue scarf which coiled shapelessly over his three jerseys and which, no matter how hard he tried, he could not get to look stylish and raffish and elegant as scarves always seemed to be on people the same build and size and age as himself. The fire hummed companionably and he sat in the chair as if drugged. Frith gazed at him affably as if about to receive from him some new admiration expressed in a more perfect and understanding language than he had ever heard before and in the small slightly dimmed eyes he sensed the voracity of one who wished by all possible means to retain that power which had once made him emperor and which in age he still had the illusion of retaining.

"I was actually expecting Robin. My son, that is," said the novelist. "He sometimes comes on a Saturday." He put the remains of his apple down, the expression on his small neat appley face not altering at all in the light of the fire, which the freezing day drove him closer to. Now and again he would appear to lose memory of his visitor as if there was something else that he wished to have which the visit was depriving him of.

"I did not catch your name," he said at last.

"Mark Simmons."

"You are a professor, perhaps?"

"No, I have lectured but I am not a professor."

"I see. I get a lot of professors. They come from Europe and America. They come from everywhere. They are writing theses on my work although I have still much to do."

Mark gazed at him as if over the rim of a hollow. This small neat dapper man, in the rays of extinction—was it truly he who had written that novel?—Those famous passages for instance about coming home at midnight through deserted streets and seeing his dead wife waiting for him at corner after corner as if duplicated by mirrors inviting him to go with her, young prostitute in all her arrogance and hauteur, into the Hades of her youth and death? No wonder the latest wife was hard and cold, competing daily against eternity, in her poor mortal skin, the queen under whose regime nothing of the slightest value had been written.

Sometimes he felt the shape of the ring in his pocket and was again stabbed by pain rising and subsiding in wave after wave as if he was in a boat.

"Tell me," he began, and stopped, petrified by a revulsion of ennui and meaninglessness. He fought his way forward through the gluey lumpish porridge of his exhaustion.

"Tell me," he said, "how long did it take you to write *A Night of Sorrows*?"

As he looked into the face, it was as if a drawbridge had suddenly been pulled up, as if he could actually see the shadows of chains on the cheeks and jaw and reflected in the eyes.

"A lot of students are writing theses about me too, but one must expect that when one reaches my age, that is, if one is any good." He pointed to a magazine which he had evidently been glancing through, if not exactly reading.

"Tell me, is Tallons any good? He seems to be very successful, appearing here and there. I must say I can't fathom him. But then that isn't uncommon with me nowadays. They write such unfinished stuff nowadays, like belisha beacons."

"I don't suppose you know Malone?" he continued. "He's trying to get me to do a book on old age. He was here not so long ago with his wife wearing corduroys, both of them actually. His wife is quite a beautiful woman. She seemed to me to be very knowledgeable as well, about certain things, you know. They all wear corduroys and demon glasses, all these American women. Not of course the sort of person you could have a discussion about Faulkner with but quite remarkably intelligent—in the way some of these American women are. We chatted about this and that and then Malone came out with this extraordinary proposal, you see. I must say that I laughed. 'Old age,' I said to him, 'What do I know about old age? I still feel like a boy'."

"Do you?" said Mark

"Do I what?"

"Feel as young as a boy?"

"Of course I do. I certainly don't feel old. What was I to say? I have lived a long time but that doesn't mean that I feel old. I can stand quite steady on my feet, converse with my children. After that we discussed a book on genealogies which I'm afraid I haven't read but Malone is very keen on. I can't stand genealogies myself. People who write stuff about genealogy seem to me to be high-powered gossips and busy-bodies. They make noseyparkerism respectable. In any case they are usually little men with bald heads who cart around with them books bigger than themselves. Extraordinary thing, Malone was wearing corduroys and sandals. I thought his feet looked a bit dirty. In my childhood I used to run about bare-foot but my feet never seemed dirty." Mark knew for a fact that Frith had been brought up in the city and wondered for a fleeting uninterested moment why he should have told the lie. "This book on genealogies has apparently been written by a man who keeps popping in and out of asylums. In the inter-vals of lucidity he writes another page and adds another foot-note."

Mark flinched and wondered. What is he thinking of me, the sparse-haired quondam lecturer in his long tweedy coat bulging with all sorts of random paraphernalia, and was about to ask him again about his first novel when a figure appeared, striding briskly past the window and in a moment entering the house.

"That's my son now," said Frith proudly. And so indeed it proved, for after some preliminary conversation with Frith's third wife—whose stepson this was—the latter entered.

He was a very clean looking man with a clear white large face and curly brown hair boyishly combed back from a tall white forehead. He wore the neat black clothes of the profes-sional and had large white bony hands which, when he sat down, he rested on his knees. He gazed at Mark in a hostile way and then turned to his father who was speaking eagerly.

"And how is the school these days? Still the efficient automaton, eh?"

"It functions," said his son briefly. "I was talking to Mrs. Mason yesterday. She said she called on you."

"That's right. She wants me to do a tape of readings from some of my prose for her classes. She's quite a bright if tiring woman."

"Yes. I have been asked myself to give a talk to the Association to explain my ideas on Secondary Education as a continuation of Primary."

"Have you? That's quite interesting. I'm very pleased. What are you going to say?"

"What I've always maintained, that one cannot have an artificial dichotomy, that there must be continuity and that there should be no interruption in the spectrum."

"And why not?" said his father who seemed to be crowing with delight. "I thought that Green . . ."

"Green? What does he know of it? His school isn't the proper size and in any case he lives in an academic dream. It seems to me indisputable that children learn through play and discovery and I see no reason why the same methods should not be applied to the Secondary School."

"You mean you don't really care whether they spell correctly or not?"

"Spelling, father, as you well know, is a recent convention. Shakespeare is supposed to have spelt his name in different ways. If Shakespeare could get along without spelling, then so can they. Not, of course, that that is desirable as long as correct spelling remains a fetish, but this may not be the case in the future."

"My son, Mr. Simmons, is very revolutionary, as you can see. He is the headmaster of a large school. I'm sure you would be interested in joining in the discussion. Mr. Simmons came to pay his respects," he said to his son.

"You are an admirer of the novel?" said the son, regarding Mark with undiminished distaste.

"I suppose you might say that," said Mark, wishing that

he could think of some devastating remark but unable to do other than sit listening to words which were meaningless to him.

"My father is all for comprehensive education in theory," said the son, "but not in practice."

"No no no, that is not what I . . ."

"In effect it is what it comes down to. Because of your socialist ideas you agree with it but your literary ideas lead you to demand perfection. I think that is the hub of it. You must go the whole hog. Perfection is not possible. The so called perfection of the academic school was a cold uninteresting one. Everyone was arranged in a rectangle facing their Socrates or rather their Solon. Now the teacher is no longer a law giver. He is himself a Columbus. Previously he knew exactly what he would find at the end of the lesson for he had put it there himself. Now he doesn't. He begins with no preconceived notions. He has no fixed ideas. He is not to be regarded as a master but as an inquirer."

His words came from him in huge slabs as from a noiseless cement mixer, the voice resonant, the convictions implacable. Curious, thought Mark, how Frith, crowing at his son's cleverness, does not see the contradiction between the positiveness of the conviction and the creative chaos of which it spoke.

"My son, you see, does not take after me," said the novelist delightedly. "He is one of our competent men. The man with the grey flannel drawers. They tell me that there is a good chance of your getting an MBE, or should I not have said that?"

"Who mentioned it to you?"

"Oh, there are rumours. Someone mentioned it to Hilda when she was shopping. My own honours will be less than yours. I was more impertinent than you and that's why only the Maori University would give me an honorary degree." He laughed joyously, with his arms around himself, an evil contorted dwarf. "By the way, that Society has asked me back again to talk to them. You know, the one where they sing 'God save the Queen' and they've got a big portrait of her behind the table and the chairman usually plays rugby on Saturdays."

"Which one is that?"

"The Rotary. They seem to have been greatly impressed by my talk. I had a nice little note from one of them. The trouble is I can't read the signature."

"Send it to the President then and explain the circumstances. He will understand."

"And I have another engagement booked in my diary for the following day. So the old man isn't doing so badly."

All this time Mark regarded the son with what might have been envy or hatred. Who are these guiltless people, he wondered, what sinless world, cold as stainless steel, have they emerged from, fully formed? They speak with conviction of the profoundest matters and what they do not speak of they consider unimportant. They have abolished or never known the past. They hum about their work like air conditioners. They believe in nothing but the adamant of themselves and yet apparently this is enough. Expecting without rancour that everyone is out to cut their throats, they get the knife in first. They are the Fortinbrases of our civilization, the clinical men who hold the cold apple in their hands and who pay a passing public homage to the antique star of an autumnal Hamlet, in the grip of its cloudy obsession. Themselves incapable of feeling, they will change from one position to another without guilt or qualm, for principles are quicksilver and obsolete. Without thinking about it, Mark said:

"Tell me, if it were suddenly laid down as a condition for professional men that they should wear their hair long, would they do so?"

He was thinking of a young boy he had seen the night before in a pub, whose body was like a tulip, the waist narrow, the head surmounted by a bulbous halo of yellow hair, thick and deep like a pelt.

There was a silence in which for the first time he heard an old grandfather clock ticking. But of course his error lay in thinking that people like the son were shakeable. No, such a question rising out of despair like a snake out of its pit had merely made him more interesting and more worth analysis.

"It would depend, I suppose," said the son thoughtfully, "on whether such a demand were consciously accepted and had an apparent justification. Yes, I suppose they would wear their hair long. After all, they wear strange gowns and hoods and were expected at certain times to discourse in Latin. What do you think, Father?"

For the first time Frith seemed to be looking at Mark with some comprehension as if he had heard in the voice the faintest vibration of pain.

"I think," he said, "if they were asked to kneel in front of a stone statue of the Buddha in order to gain their certificates they would do so, but they would justify it."

Mark, turning the ring over and over in his hand, was still watching the son who had apparently dismissed the question from his lovely and unclouded conscience, for he had begun to say:

"Hilda was saying that you have been sent a translation of one of your books into Finnish. Is that right? That's something new, surely."

"Yes, quite new. But another strange thing happened this week as well. Apparently Jerry—do you remember Jerry Dalgleish?—is in town again."

"I thought he was in Nigeria."

"No, he's back. They didn't like his writings over there either. Of all things, he wants me to write an introduction to that biography he's been working on now for the last fifteen years. He says he's finished it. Some obscure publisher has agreed to do it. What do you think I should do?"

"Oh, don't do it of course if you don't want to."

"But he's in pretty low straits and he's depending on this . . ."

"In that case . . . Still, would it do your reputation any good?"

"I don't think it would do it any harm. No-one's likely to read the book anyway."

"Well, do it then. He may not get it published anyway. By

the way, I was speaking to a great admirer of yours the other day."

"Oh? Who?"

"The father of one of my pupils. He said he was standing beside you in a pub once and you, not of course knowing him, proceeded to give him a long discourse on Hemingway. He thought it very charming of you and says he learnt a lot. I wish some of the knowledge could be rubbed off on his son."

"How extraordinary. And I can't even remember it. I find I can hardly remember anything that happened to me after the age of thirty. Isn't that odd?" he said to Mark. "I was reading an article the other day in which the writer maintained that my later work is much better than my earlier."

"I am sure Mr. Simmons agrees," said the son negligently.

"No, I don't."

"Oh, why not?"

Mark was about to elaborate when he realised that the son did not care one way or another, but that his mind—which never forgot anything, he was sure—would have assembled from various periodicals and scattered lectures enough facts to maintain an obtuse and ultimately barren argument in which neither could communicate with the other. So he said nothing.

At that moment Hilda came to the door, glancing at him casually as if to say, "Are you still here?" She said, "I'm going down to the shops for some meat. Can I take your car?" she said to the son.

"Of course."

"And bring back a bottle of whisky," said her husband gaily. She ignored him as if she had heard that pleasantry many times before and then said to the son:

"By the way, I see that friend of yours writing in the *Spectator* again."

"Oh you mean Maitland. Yes, he's doing quite well."

"I suppose he finds English education quite different," said his father. "When I was young there was no nonsense. The only streams we ever knew anything about were streams of piss."

The vulgarity, delivered casually in the cosy amber-coloured room, by the small toylike man, was as shocking to Mark as if the small leaded window had been shattered by a stone, but Hilda only laughed and pulled the door to and Mark could hear her walking over the frosty ground to the car.

He began to think of leaving but as so often happened with him found it difficult to stand up and actually go. The vagueness of his pretext for being there—an open-mouthed adoring consultation of the oracle, the expectation of a monologue dense with wisdom and knowledge of life—made his departure so much harder to accomplish as if he felt that perhaps there was even yet a faint chance of communication beyond the parochial chit-chat to which he had been listening. He had wanted the novelist to talk about that early novel—which constituted in fact the only indisputably great work he had ever accomplished both by the intensity of the feeling and the bravura of the imagery—but as he was apparently no longer the man who had written it, no longer the man able to listen unafraid to the voices from another world which commemorated the wife both hated and loved, there was little point in staying. But, before he could leave, the son had said:

"And how are your rabbits getting on these days?"

"Oh fine, fine. Beautifully. I did write a note to thank Lena for them. The boys will be over to see them again soon."

"Yes," said the old man suddenly. "I must say that I agree with that writer. My later work *is* better, and shall I tell you why? Because I am in control of it. And that is as good a reason as any. Not to be in control is bad. In my early work I wrote about ghosts that did not exist. I know why you've come," he said to Mark, "you want me to go over and over that agony. Well, I won't. Not for you and not for anyone else. I regret ever publishing that book. Bitterly. It's a psychological document, not a novel."

He pointed his finger at Mark. "That's why you came, isn't it? I'm no fool and I have a life to live. You go on living yours. That's your job."

The son looked from one to the other in an amused detached

way. "I don't know what all this is supposed to be about but I do know that you are supposed to take your tablets at about this time, aren't you?"

The little old man smiled delightedly and said:

"I'd hoped you would have forgotten. But then you're used to timetables and shit like that."

The son went to another room and returned with some tablets and a tumbler of water.

"Come on now. Knock them down. You want to live for another twenty years, don't you?"

"Certainly I want to live. Who doesn't? Even rats want to live." As he was about to swallow them he said, "You know, a dream keeps coming back to me. I'm sitting on the upper deck of a tram and there are leaves trailing down the window. We're going down an avenue, you see. And the tram is all glass like your schools and politicians' heads. And I'm sitting up there by myself wearing shorts and some kind of chain. There doesn't seem to be anyone on the tram—not even a conductor—and yet I've got a ticket. Anyway, we're driving along—there are no rails either—and I see ahead of me a small statue crowned in flowers. Only this side of it there's this girl who's turning up her bottom at me in a mocking sort of way. I'm sure it must have some deep meaning."

Mark levered himself to his feet, like a rusty cannon, tightening his belt on his coat as he did so.

"Must be going now," he mumbled.

Four eyes like torches glared at him. He felt himself subsumed in their different intelligences.

"Pleased to have met you," he mumbled.

The son politely accompanied him to the door, watching him as he trudged along to the bus-stop. Mark then heard the door being shut behind him though he did not turn round to see.

Through the waste gloomy day the bus plodded on, Mark sitting in a front seat, his hands deep in his tweedy pockets, pulling his coat tight about him. They passed cottages at which long-skirted women stood waving: they headed towards a sun the colour of rum straddling the road. Nothing leaped out at him. There was merely leather (on which he sat), conversation (which he half overheard), the held picture of the novelist and son in a light the colour of brandy, a Dutch house clean and neat and caged.

His gaze rested on the driver's massive head fixed to the hairy red neck, like a stone ball one sometimes sees perched on top of a gatepost. He thought of him driving day after day, night after night, very stiff, very upright, consistently making allowances for the crazy little drivers he saw below him careering hither and thither. Lorna could drive, crazily too, lovably clumsy, capable of breaking cup after cup. The driver, large and still, was responsible for them all, never perhaps even thinking about it, as was fitting.

"I have nowhere to go," some voice was saying deep within him and he listened to it as a radio astronomer might listen to the single piercing note—enough to vibrate glass—from outer space, telling of a distant star not visible to the naked eye and taken on trust. In his mind he turned the statement over and over—starry like a broken window—like a jeweller examining a stone. There had been Lorna and then before that there had been his parents and now there was nothing but the statement, "I have nowhere to go." He felt much as an astronaut might feel, spinning crazily about the cabin of his ship headed for the moon or Mars, disoriented, head and body pointed in no particular direction that one could name in the depths of space.

Open space now began to be filled with blocks of buildings —a hospital, a school, a block of flats—the beginnings of the city. Orange street lamps with flat viperish heads illuminated the roadway studying their own haloes. People laden with packages scurried across the road, and women in hoods entered and left the bus. He thought vaguely and without interest of the Christmas Cards which were sure to be lying in the lobby of the house. For a moment his mind blacked out and he thought of what he should buy for Lorna. His eyes smarted but remained dry: he locked his teeth together. By now the novelist and his son—a title to remind one of Dickens: why

Dickens? Was it because of the Christmas associations and the sprig of holly he had seen lying on top of a magazine in the house?—would be immersed in their chatter. Why had he gone to visit Frith at all? It had been an action he could not rationally construe except of course for those months spent on the unfinished book about him, unfinished like the long labour of the man—Dalgleish, was it?—from Nigeria. He was shaken by a pain which started in his stomach and spread all round him, a real pain, a feeling at the same time of being dissociated and floating in space.

The novelist—great untidy star—had hatched a star purer and colder than himself, casting the light of education with controlled discrimination all over the cold earth.

That early novel of his where he had once walked with the blue light rushing from the abyss at his feet, these passages about a woman, careful of each emotion and measuring them out in doses, belonged to another man whose body was now immune to the onset of ghosts or passions.

"What price my lecturing now?" he thought. "What price my Eliot and my Dante? Little Simmons, centre of the cosmic universe, what price your Eliot now?"

He stumbled out of the bus and began to walk. The snow glared back at him as he walked, collar hunched up, into the keen wind, passing at a corner a group of students in long blue scarves gathered round a brazier and a large notice which told the literate world—burdened under its Christmas parcels— that they were on a forty-eight hour fast for Biafra. Their drama—inside which they themselves huddled: would they at the end of the forty-eight hours have a good large dinner in a good large warm restaurant and then go home to sleep together, perhaps in a good large warm bed?—meant nothing to him, or rather they seemed, like everyone else, to be acting out a public part which had no relation to anything his mind could seriously fasten on. He walked past them without stopping, a hunched up forty-two year old with scuffy brown shoes and a brown hat and a face beaten against by the bitter wind.

The snow reflected an eerie glow such as one might find on the surface of a planet immune to life, its whiteness emerging without pretext from the night, unlike any other whiteness that one could conceive of, unlike for instance the whiteness of cotton or wool or Rinso or the foam of waves, inhuman, unable to be made use of, merely a visitation that, as queer as manna, dropped out of the sky. "A journey and such a long journey." He felt the desire to urinate just as he saw an arrow pointing to a Gents which was at the foot of a flight of slippery steps. He descended—letting his body go—and entered the place all white and marbly and lit with a garish light. He looked at his face in a mirror and tried to adjust his scarf for the tenth time, feeling Lorna's phantom hands on it and screwing his face up tight. He weighed himself on the weighing machine, digging down to the lining for a threepenny bit. Ten stone and, "YOU SHOULD TAKE RISKS THIS WEEKEND. YOUR LOVE LIFE WILL GO WELL". The lavatory offered a brush-up service and he found a small hunched monosyllabic man with a pail and mop.

"Sixpence for a brush-up," said the man morosely as if it wasn't quite the right thing for people to be taking brush-ups in lavatories at all, rather like cleaning women who get angry if there is anything to clean. Mark, raked by contempt, pulled the door shut behind him, removed his hat and coat and, sticking a paper towel down behind his jersey, began to shave, having taken from his bulging pocket the shaving bag with its brush, palmolive shaving cream, and green topped capsule of styptic. The small room he was in looked inhuman and dead like a fish-shop—he half expected to see the dead cold eye of a cod on a slab—a refuge for whiskery and whiskied men and he was suddenly frightened as if the steps by which he had descended were symbolic of another descent. "I am forty-two," he thought, "what is there left for me?" Up until now he had not felt forty-two: in fact he couldn't think what age he must have felt, perhaps an eternal nineteen as he was in that picture which hung in the kitchen showing him with bright ready eyes, wavy brown hair, a matching striped scarf and tie, and a smile which slightly inflated the cheeks. That had been taken

23

in his student days when he would write flippant notes on the backs of photographs like "a distant relation of Darwin". Then there had been the photograph with the two girls—one dark and one blonde—who sat placidly, hands on laps at the front, while he and David, now an engineer, stood behind, hands resting lightly on the girls' shoulders.

He washed in the warm water and arranged his clothes again. He gave the man sixpence, and again felt, deep within, shaken by desolate tremors. The surly caretaker hardly spoke when Mark offered him the placatory news that it was a cold night outside as if the payment of the sixpence were not in itself enough. He merely grunted and carried his pail another few feet along. Mark entered the cold air again. He had no idea where he was going: all places were of equal value and therefore valueless. The red lights of cinemas flashed on and off all round him, and off to his right he saw the fairy castle tenderly illuminated and appearing like a large ghost in the white light. What Mark wanted above all was a warm place where he could sit and not actually freeze and when he came to a large theatre he entered it as the wind might enter a close.

He sat in his seat—one of the very few occupied ones on the balcony—and stared, flinty-faced, into the arena below him, curtained as yet, since the precise time for beginning the show had not arrived. Most of the time he shivered uninterruptedly, now and again gazing with lacklustre eyes and a face that seemed polished by the cold at the little plaster angels in the corners of the roof, all blowing their plaster trumpets. The encounter in the lavatory had upset him. He imagined the Welfare State as a cosy bubble out of which he was being slowly squeezed like toothpaste out of a tube. He thought of the whiskery men he had seen in reading rooms here and there huddled in their large trailing coats, turning over page after page but reading nothing.

Eventually, as he gazed, a microphone appeared in front of the curtain and the comic, in maxi coat, flat cap on head, danced out of the left wing of the stage.

"Nice shed you got here," he said and there was approving

laughter, the audience wishing to show that they were not provincial enough to be offended.

"Listen," he said urgently, "I flew here. I flew here. My arms are sore yet. But, listen, there was this wain running up and down the corridor of the plane, the corridor of the plane, this wee wain, and I said to him, 'Sonny, why don't you go outside and play?' That's better. You're paying for it. Might as well enjoy it. Might as well lean back and enjoy it as the bishop said to the actress. It's better than being at home with the kids. Listen, this'll slay you. Last night I told the wife I was coming here today, I said to her, 'I'm going to the North Pole tomorrow,' I told the wife that and I said to her, 'I'd like toast and tea and a boiled egg. Don't forget,' I said to her, 'toast and tea and a boiled egg.' Well this morning, sure enough, she came in with the toast. Then she went out and a few minutes later she came back with the boiled egg. So after a while I waited and waited and waited but there was no tea. So I shouted to her, 'Where's the tea? Where's the tea?' I shouted to her. 'What happened to the tea?' And do you know what she said, do you know what she said? She said, 'The electricity's been off all morning.' And do you know what? I'm still wondering how she boiled the egg."

Jaunty and perky and keeping smiling, the comic cradled the microphone in his two hands, leaning into it as if he were speaking to a lover, sometimes stepping backward in his maxi coat to execute a miniature dance and pouring out joke after joke to which the audience, puppet-like, responded with shouts of laughter which sounded almost like snarls.

"I'll tell you," he said, "if you took all the coloured people out of Britain we'd have an extra hour of daylight. But see, this is Christmas time, isn't it? Isn't it? Christmas. Well, I'll tell you a Christmas story. This woman went to steal from a shop, see, from a shop. She'd take a pair of panties and she'd stuff them down here"—indicating the left side of his breast—"and then, see, she'd take another pair"—his voice was hushed now—"and she'd stuff them down here"— indicating the right side of his breast. Well, there was this supervisor and she saw this happening, this supervisor, a big, fat woman, and as the thief was going out the door she shouted to her. 'Hey, come back here with that chest of drawers.' Great what people will do at Christmas, init?"

To the left of him Mark saw three unmarried women—un-ringed at any rate—sitting together, helplessly laughing and gazing at each other with sidelong glances as if to make sure that the other two were laughing as well. One of them reminded him of Mrs. Walton. At that moment the comic burst into song. "The Bonnie Lass of Ballochmyle" sung with throbbing voice and inflated red cheeks (puffed out like balloons) soared to the roof and raised with it (to the plaster angels) girls, men, boys, all who had come into the circle of light from the outer darkness and the eerie snow, all who existed from moment to moment, those who had stumbled down frosty steps and those who had not, including the flat-capped comic himself.

He remembered how he and Lorna would sometimes watch "Dixon of Dock Green" on the telly and her delighted laugh when he'd salute at the end after his bit of moralising was over, his face serious and respectful and worn with defending the public from his cut-price, shoddy, mindless villains. She waited for this moment all week, dragging Mark in from his book; sometimes she'd only put on that bit with the salute and nothing else, so endearing was it in its old world innocence, so different from the hard, real efficiency of "Softly, Softly" where everybody devoured everybody else.

He passed his hand across his eyes. The comic, like life, was still there, insisting on being noticed, his voice hoarse from telling the same jokes over and over in theatre after theatre, shouting into the darkness which erupted now and again with laughter and, like the sound of shore water, showing that he was still in contact with land; still surviving, that in the middle of the howling waters his light was still flashing. What would Lorna have made of this? Perhaps she would have liked it. She still had that childish quality of those who, quite innocent of cruelty, like to see the man with the umbrella slipping on the banana skin in the radiant day when the street is full of light

26

and sparkling bicycle wheels and men leaning down outside shops to examine boxes of oranges and apples or sharpening their knives in butchers' shops.

He himself had liked the Goons and the Monty Python Show —those comedies which existed in incoherencies and hints and unfinished ideas taken up and dropped as carelessly as Lorna might drop a cup or a plate and he might say "Oh, not again," the endearing clumsiness not so much a joke, and she would look at him in a queer way, sometimes laughing it off, sometimes beginning a shrill quarrel. Strange how these shows, admired for their incoherences—as of life itself, not art— seemed more threatening and prophetic, now that he himself was existing from moment to moment, one of the many into whose face a microphone might be thrust in the middle of the street to elicit for the bright eyed interviewer a contribution not from a human being but a type, a type as funny and pathetic as himself, or that comic who was now telling a sick joke about somebody's grandmother which was interrupted from behind Mark by the pure gay crystal laugh of a child, not perhaps as a consequence of the joke but simply a spark of spontaneous self-delighting joy such as he himself had often felt when young, creeping conspiratorially about the house, where his parents were still lying asleep.

He rose suddenly and made his way down the large plushy empty stairs past the woman at the desk in the foyer who was polishing her nails and into the large white night whose coldness immediately struck him in the face. He trudged along— he had never learned to drive a car, though Lorna, in spite of her clumsiness, had—and he came to a pub which he entered. He ordered a rum to keep out the cold and stood around the wooden trough inside which the white-coated barman was.

He looked around him but there was no-one he knew and he felt again the warning inner trembling. There were pairs of men in discussion amid clouds of smoke, and students discussing examinations on the leather seats running round the room. The door of the lavatory was decorated with holly, and he thought this rather funny as he sipped his rum, feeling its radiant coils running all round his body. He took it over to a table and sat down.

He thought of their last holiday and how they'd sit on a bench by the sea in that small town inhabited by retired left-overs of a vanished empire, living on their pensions, being taken out for walks by their slim yellow dogs, and how for the first time the Fair had managed to break its way in, with its outdated music-hall decor, its little cars, and the man standing straddle-legged in the middle while the children shouted and screamed.

He remembered watching her from the ground as she drove her little car round and round, bumping into a large stolid man with a moustache who smiled and waved, with a large cigar in his mouth. He saw her mouth forming words which because of the music and the shouting he could not hear. He heard himself making some remark about bingo as later they walked along in the calm evening, she stopping now and then to spin a flat stone across the water, a trick which she had learned somewhere on her travels.

The last night they had been there had been a really beautiful one with a red sky ahead of them and shops illuminated by it casting their shadows in the water where children played with dogs. The tide was at its fullest, covering the black wiry tangle of seaweed with a silken smoothness. The young girls walked to their assignations and he thought that Lorna looked at them with a certain sadness. Once two girls in green on horseback clattered down the street and he had made some remark to Lorna only to find that she was not listening but was following them with an intense yet abstracted gaze. The night held the first taste of autumn, a hint of iciness. He felt—reading his spy story—that Lorna shivered a little and told her without raising his head that she should put her scarf on. They had talked—or rather Lorna had talked—to an old man who was ninety-six years old with all his faculties intact and could remember the days when that town had been connected with the city twenty miles away by a tram line. Lorna was interested in all that, asking questions, some stupid, some not, while he himself had read on in his book, throwing it when finished into the green bin at the side of the seat.

He bought another rum and sipped it slowly.

"I said you're very quiet. Don't you want to speak to me?" said the drunk scarfed man sitting in front of him at the opposite end of the table.

"Don't you want to speak to me? I'm not good enough for you, am I? Is that it? Eh?"

"I'm sorry," said Mark automatically (he had noticed often that if he hadn't been listening to what someone was saying he would say, "I'm sorry"). "I'm sorry. I didn't see you."

"Didn't see me, eh? That's no excuse. You haven't answered my question. That's no answer to my question."

"I didn't hear you ask a question."

The fuddled eyes bore up slowly like a howitzer being levered and the mouth said:

"No excuse. Not see me, eh? Not good enough for you, am I? That's what you said. And you didn't answer my question. Why didn't you answer my question? Not good enough for you, eh?"

The monotonous inanity of the drunk jarred and at the same time threatened him. He rose and stood over at the other side of the bar watching the drunk who was pawing vaguely at some money which had fallen to the floor. On an impulse he bought him a drink and laid it on the table beside him. The drunk looked at him as if from underwater and then deliberately (he was sure it was done deliberately) upset the drink all over the floor. "Don' wan' charity," he said, "wan' you to talk to me." Mark stood there for a moment trying to think of something to say, while the barman in silence came over with a cloth and wiped the table. Then he left.

A hotel. He needed a bed, he needed a room of his own, a place in which he could draw the curtains and turn the key in the lock. A hotel. That was it. A room where he could sleep after he had taken his pills to quieten the drum that was steadily beating in his head. The door swung two or three times behind him as he left.

2

The hotel, though from the front it appeared small, turned out to have a large number of rooms. The number on his key was 501. It was given to him at the desk by a pallid girl in a gold miniskirt while behind, swinging her legs on a chair, was another who was saying into a phone: "Certainly, Mr. Dixon, a table for two. On the 27th you said." The hotel did not give the impression of great business but he remembered that it was Christmas-time when all self-respecting people would be with their families drinking their sherry or port or whisky, when dour-looking Scrooges like himself ought to be behind chained doors peering rancorously at the carol singers. A porter conducted him (with his orange case which he had retrieved from the left luggage at the station) into the lift which deposited him on the fifth floor not far from the door of his room. There seemed to be no-one on the landing but himself and he familiar-ised himself with the position of the Toilet and the Bathroom before entering the room and locking the door. It was like any other hotel room with a bed with a pink counterpane, an old wardrobe, a dressing chest, a wash basin with a rack for hand towel and bath towel, and amber-coloured curtains which did not quite reach the floor. The hotel's insignia were stamped on the mirror (would anyone steal a mirror?)

He lay down on the bed fully clothed and shut his eyes, hearing from outside the roar of the traffic, and from the hotel itself the movement of feet and the rushing of lavatory water. After a while he sat up and looked at his watch—a present from Lorna—which told him it was eight thirty. He decided to go to bed, and undressing and shivering, put on a pair of clean pyjamas he took from his case. He noticed that there was a hole in his sock and, not knowing what to do about it, smiled sourly. He laid his clothes over the back of the chair, not bothering to use the wardrobe. The coat clinked hollowly with coins and keys and the ring, which he had at one stage put into an empty aspirin bottle but, the bottle breaking and cutting his hand, he had removed the ring and left it in his pocket.

He put out the light and lay back on the bed. In the darkness of the room he felt for a moment as if Lorna was present, emerged from the darkness, but his heart-beat quietened after a while. She had been used to hotels before she married him, travelling all over the world in her affluent harum-scarum way, inheriting much money from her desiccated aunts and uncles who always seemed to be on ocean liners while she was packed off to schools here and there. Once she had sent him a letter written in a large round scrawl from one of these liners, off hand, vivid in spite of or because of the negligence, feverish describing the correct officers and the old ladies with their sticks and smoked glasses leaning back in their cane chairs. But since then they hadn't been in hotels much: in fact he was little used to them, was in fact much less at ease than she would have been when, in her large-gestured way, she would have all the waiters at her feet, because she, after all, was one of the chosen ones, conversant with all the right knives and forks and spoons and serviettes, by training long become instinct, and she would treat them with the casual effrontery that they immediately recognised as if by application of a tuning fork.

That had been their first quarrel when he had said that she must take no money from anyone but him, not from her relatives, not from anyone, and she had looked at him first with surprise and then with love. He had thought that the battle would be a bitter one—he with his dour Calvinist conscience—furniture pared to the bare minimum, as indeed, he reflected amusedly, the furniture in the hotel room was: and the battle had been fought in the hard light of the as yet unshaded bulbs in the house he had bought or at least had begun to pay for. (He remembered the two of them, with ladders and paste, scraping walls into the late pale hours of midnight, she wearing the blue slacks which she wore when painting.) The fight had not been as hard as he had thought it would be, or at least at the time it did not appear hard. He had been prepared for a savage rending duel—but no, she had given in and had then gone on to glance through a copy of *Woman* or some such magazine which at that time she used to hunt through for recipes, and whose love stories she also read with great interest, while he himself, of course, read the *Statesman and Nation* and the *Listener*. Even now he could see her—legs outstretched in front of her—glancing rapidly and with her quick nervousness through the magazine. She never read much and nothing very deep.

As he lay there in the darkness he saw straight ahead of him, suspended above the cold city, a huge Christmas tree between the two open curtains one of which was drooping from one corner, and thought of the hermit whom Lorna and Mrs. Carmichael had in unison invaded and begun to help, a substitute perhaps for feeding the starving in Biafra or Vietnam. (He himself after a period of liberalism found himself going over to the side of the conservatives who wrote regularly in the *Spectator* attacking the leftist liberals.) The balloons on the tree swayed in a slight breeze and the lights flickered on and off.

The Christmas tree—ornate as it was—seemed to comfort him, to companion him in the otherwise dark night. He imagined for a moment what it might be really like—a tree with on it the crucified Jesus with slack yellow legs as in mediaeval paintings and the head with its crown of thorns fallen inertly on the narrow chest. His mind shied away from the concatenation of images—the crown, the sponge, the vinegar—and steadied on the lighted tree. He remembered just before leaving the house finding underneath a pile of clothes the Christmas card she had been going to send him, an abstract angel descending over an abstract crib. She liked Christmas for there was a lot of the child in her. She liked buying presents and dressing up: her wandering extravagant childhood had seen to that. She liked surprising him with cufflinks and scarves (which he said she ought not to have bought) and handkerchiefs of pure white Irish linen. At Christmas time she was for ever rushing to the letter box (her hearing was much better than his) and coming back with her cards. She was always sending cards to people she had known but briefly, people who had been at various schools with her, acquaintances even (if she could discover their addresses). One of their few friends was a bachelor—a lecturer in History, a spectacled, dry man—who never sent cards on principle (he had taken up Hinduism instead) and she couldn't understand this at all, she distrusted him instinctively.

"I'm sure his Hinduism has something to do with his being a bachelor," Lorna would say. She came out with sudden flashes like that which disconcerted him, made him a little wary of her, which made him wonder perhaps whether in her own wandering disorganised way she might not be brighter than himself.

It was strange to find that he—the arch disbeliever, the one who never sent Christmas cards—should in this small room be comforted by the Christmas tree with all its swaying coloured worlds. At the level at which he lay there was nothing else that he could see. The thin skins of the big balloons swayed in the high wind. Lorna had been afraid of storms. One night after returning from a useless boring departmental meeting he had found her huddled inside a cupboard while sheet lightning illuminated the room and a window banged, she having been afraid to shut it. He had been a long time quietening her down, but had eventually laughed it off, seeing it as a joke.

"It's no joke to me," she had said. However, in the radiant morning which followed the storm she was happy again moving among the modernities of her kitchen.

She had a long time ago insisted on a Christmas tree, though he didn't like such things. Her liking for Christmas seemed to him to be on a par with her reading of *Woman's Own* with every appearance of pleasure which to his *New Statesman* mind (slightly stained by the *Spectator*) was like coming across a Wasp in his living room. (He would have had more respect for her if she had learned to read *Nova*, which was at least literate.) Yet she loved these stories of nurses and doctors in hospitals, concerned with their own love affairs more than with their patients. She was immune to the barbaric prose which he could not read without retching and she'd say to him:

"What's wrong with you is that you aren't human. Really."

"It's because I am human that I can't stand that Christmassy junk."

Then there had been that argument with that uncle of hers, who raised cattle in the South of England after making money in the diamond mines in Africa and later on in oil in Saudi Arabia where apparently one was not allowed to drink alcoholic liquors at all.

"I am afraid," the uncle had said amiably after a while—he had, against Mark's better judgment taken them out to the sort of classy hotel where the manager would turn out a diner unless he was wearing a tie and had ordered among other things a fine white wine which Mark didn't like—"I am afraid I am all for apartheid," and had gone on to tell a story about taking a camera off at the customs, only to be stopped by an obstreperous native official who had insisted on seeing how it was used, thus holding up a crowd of people.

"They are really pretty childish, you know," he had said comfortably, his white shirt glittering in the light. (Mark was wearing a yellow polo-necked jersey but so far no-one had come to put him out.) A lot of the time the uncle had kept up a running badinage with the initially aloof waitress who had unbent enough to tell them something about her life, an auto-biography which Mark deplored. The gift of a pound to her at the end seemed to Mark rather excessive though perhaps it had been related to the free view the uncle got of her thighs when she was bending over an adjacent table arranging the cutlery. Everything about that night made him angry, the affluent carelessness of the uncle, the obvious enjoyment Lorna took in his company, the in-jokes between the two of them, the ease with which the uncle ordered the food and knew exactly what he wanted.

"It's all very well for people like you to talk," Mark had said heatedly, "But, after all, that country doesn't belong to you. It belongs to the Africans themselves. That's what you seem to forget. What god-given right have you to go over there and milk these people of everything they have?"

The uncle—a large smiling man who spooned trifle into his mouth with the greatest pleasure and delight—had continued to eat for some time without answering and then had said:

"Tell me, do you yourself mix with the 'lower classes'?"

Lorna had laughed: "Of course he doesn't. He doesn't mix with anybody. Not anybody and this is true. He mixes only with himself." It didn't matter what she wore, she always looked as if she were dressed in a painter's smock.

"That has nothing to do with it," said Mark heatedly. "I don't take anything away from the lower classes. I don't limit their freedom. They are allowed equal education which they aren't in African countries."

The uncle remained infuriatingly silent for a while as if he were wondering how anyone could put forward such ridiculously naive arguments, saying in the interval that he hoped the conversation wasn't boring Lorna. Then he said carelessly:

"Of course you know they are quite ineducable. Please believe me, I have been among them. When I went out there I was just as liberal as you. You're not the only one who reads the *Statesman*, you know. We all do, some of us for fun. However, experience taught me differently. They are quite unable to pick up anything. That's why their planes are being blown out of the sky by the Israelites, for instance. Now there is a race I admire."

"Just like me," said Lorna, "absolutely unmechanical. Do you know, Uncle Edward, that I had the most hellish time with the cooker and Mark here wasn't much better."

"We all know," said Mark furiously (he always preferred to trade more in ideas than in facts) "how the educational budget is distributed."

"You know it from biased sources," said the uncle wiping his cleanshaven chin with a napkin. "You haven't been there so you can't know. Please don't think I'm being heavy handed, only realistic. Their minds work differently from ours. Now don't think that I deduce from this that we are superior to them: I'm not saying that at all. All I'm saying is that they're different. Shall I tell you a story? Once they were issued with

35

wheelbarrows. And do you know what they did? They went about carrying them on their heads. They used to say: things were easier here before the white man came. And that's what our friend Wilson calls the white heat of the technological revolution." He laughed loudly and pleasantly and infectiously so that two men sitting silently by themselves turned and looked at them, as if wishing that they could join in the conversation.

"You shouldn't laugh at them," said Lorna. "I know that you taught me horse riding but you shouldn't laugh at them. I hope you're going to stay the night but you mustn't laugh at them."

But the uncle hadn't stayed the night though his intention had at first been precisely this. In fact, he had decided to sell his farm and go abroad again.

"I'm going to make a gesture," he said. "I'm going to Rhodesia."

"Oh," said Mark, coldly abandoning him.

"Yes, that's what I'm going to do. I believe in my principles. In any case the climate over there is better and I can afford it." He had also insisted on paying the bill which had been rather a large one. All in all, it hadn't been a successful evening, Mark not liking the uncle at all, mainly because of his large easy confidence and especially because of the cards which he carried in his wallet with his name, address, and telephone number.

"You like it here?" he had said to Lorna. She had looked at him for a long time and then said, "Yes, uncle, I do. It's beautiful." There was a haunting quality in the admission which had caused the uncle to sigh briefly and then say:

"I remember a long time ago you said the same about London. You were always on about these homosexual artists who bought flowers for each other. Fabulous was the word you used, I believe."

"Yes," Lorna said quietly, "That was the word I used."

"I see. In that case, perhaps I could buy you another drink before we part for a while."

But Mark wanted to go home, and Lorna had followed

with her eyes the large easy uncle making his way to the lift as if she would never see him again.

"He tried to teach me horse riding," she said to Mark as he thought rather irrelevantly, "he was very patient. I never did learn but he did try to teach me."

That night Lorna had been very distant and quiet as if blaming him for getting rid of the uncle of whom she appeared so very fond.

"He doesn't think much of a simple lecturer," said Mark.

"Oh, he's got a great respect for learning," said Lorna, pulling off her stockings, "And he reads a lot. His wife's dead, you know. He thought a lot of her." She looked pale in the half darkness of the room, like a fish in the shadowed part of a stream.

"Anyway, your book will be good and they'll make you a senior lecturer or something fabulous like that. Then you can teach Eliot all the time."

"Here? I don't want to stay here."

"So you say. But you've been here a long time."

"I should have thought that you would have been the last to want to stay here," said Mark petulantly, opening the window slightly and feeling the fat scent of the flowers on the night air. "I haven't been anywhere."

"Yes, but that was necessity," she said slipping her dress over her head.

Suddenly she came over and put her arms around him without saying anything, clutching him tightly, almost like a child, her lips cold and dry.

But he was still angry about the uncle: "Damn fool," he muttered. And then gaily, "He'll end up with a white moustache and a red face, like all of them."

"Of course you know that he's got an M.C." she said, her voice muffled. "He won it in Libya, I believe. I can't remember it very well but it was to do with getting someone out of a burning tank. Mind you, he used to drink a lot after he came home from the war."

"He missed the killing, I suppose."

"No. It wasn't that. He always used to tell my father that he should make more of himself instead of living off his money. Daddy inherited a lot of money, you know. But he's never done a stroke in his life. He goes about like the Duke of Windsor, very bored, but always telling everyone he's happy."

"And does your mother look like the Duchess of Windsor?"

"My mother is very beautiful. She once asked me if I had been deflowered yet. That was when I was sixteen and she seemed disappointed when I said I hadn't. She thought it was unhealthy or something. Very hygienic, my mother." She laughed loudly and gaily.

"He's a very efficient man, my uncle," she continued. "He runs his farm like clockwork. Everything he tries he does well. I envy that in people, don't you?"

"No," said Mark unnecessarily loudly, "It depends what they're doing, I'd say."

They went to bed. She came closer to him, putting her arms around him and he was suddenly flooded by an extraordinary happiness and desire which left him almost weak.

"You were supposed to die for us," said Mark to himself looking out at the Christmas tree. "You were supposed to save us. But it's no good, she took the ring from her finger." The hot water wheezed in the pipes.

After the snow and the shivering he thought of the brown land where Christ had walked in his long white robe and long hair, blessing, gathering disciples, the blue sea never far away. He imagined Frith's son saying, "Educate. Everything is possible," and Christ carrying a wheelbarrow on his head. The meek head—with the weight of the inexpressible—bowed before the Pilate to whom all things are expressible and that which was inexpressible did not exist.

On and off flashed the light of the Christmas tree as on and off flashed the images in his mind. High up in the night he eventually slept, stretching his arm out now and again in his sleep and finding nothing, and the embrace of nothing teaching him the new habit of not stretching out. Ahead of him the light flickered on and off, throughout the night.

To rise in the morning involved the most terrible effort: this must be, he thought, what it must be like to wake in a capsule, far from earth, all communications gone. Connected to reality by his watch which said eight o'clock, he struggled into his clothes as if against a high wind. Deep inside him a negative star was pulsing destructive signals: he was tuned into anti-matter. It kept saying—that jagged star—"Lie down. There is no point. You have nowhere to go. You are yourself alone and that is nothing." His eyes seemed to be, without knowing it, searching the room for a powder puff, a compact, anything that might speak of her but there was only alien impersonality. The pulsing star seemed to be whispering death in his ear. To stand upright was to be like the first man, descended from the companionable trees, balancing himself in a morning without promise.

"I must eat," he thought, "that is what I must do." He shaved and dressed quickly and went into the dining room for breakfast which was served by a boy with long hair in off-white stained uniform. He passed the night porter's place where there were newspapers on sale and he realised that he hadn't read a newspaper for a week. He could do without all that. What he had to do was survive. With a frozen face he ate his porridge—which Lorna could not abide—and his ham and egg, cramming it down against all inclination. Then he paid his bill and left the hotel with his orange case. It was still very cold. Where now? he wondered. He felt he had to polish his shoes and descended the steps to the station again where there was no brown shoe polish, only black. He passed the bookstall—where they were advertising Updike's *Couples*—without buying anything, and at the ticket office bought a ticket for the northern city at which he had attended university. An irate ticket collector shunted him to the right platform and he sat down in a corner seat in one of the leading carriages. A soldier in khaki passed the window and a phantom memory of barracks and cold water and targets jagged his mind for a moment. Once he had been travelling on a train—a sergeant in the Intelligence Corps—when he had got into conversation with a young ATS girl whom he had on the spur of the moment asked to go out with him. "Phone me," she had said, "I work on the switchboard." As if she hadn't believed that he would go out with her. But he hadn't phoned her after all.

A woman as small as a toy sat down on the seat opposite him. The train jolted backwards and forwards but did not start. He looked dully out of the window at the landscape of grey stone, hugging himself in the corner because of the cold. The train moved and objects which before had been here were now there. He closed his eyes.

"Would you like a Victory V?" said the little woman, offering him a glazed red packet. "To keep off the cold."

He took it, snuggling more deeply into his corner. "Have you escaped the flu?" she said perhaps noticing some signs of ravage and recent wreckage in his pale face. He heard himself saying that he had indeed escaped the flu and asking her if she had.

"Oh I'm just after an operation," she said. "For my veins, you see. The doctor said I'd be dead else. The blood wasn't getting through, you see. We live in Glasgow—my man and me—near Castlemilk. Perhaps you've heard of Castlemilk? When I say 'Castlemilk' people stare. But we don't stay in Castlemilk itself. My son now, he hates Glasgow—he's a carpenter by trade—he gets out of it any chance he can. Loves the country, you understand. My neighbour—that's Mrs. Mason—she thought I was going to die, honest." The little woman laughed delightedly. "It was a big operation, I can tell you. The doctor said I could have passed away. They had to open up my veins. But I feel great now. I told the kids—that's the grandchildren—I would be jigging at their Christmas Party and I will too, I feel so great. Before, I couldn't drag myself about. I was in a chair all the time. What sort of life was that? So when I got the chance I took it."

Mark stared at her as if at a being from another world, not speaking but quite glad to hear her talk.

"I go up there every Christmas. There's nothing like Christmas with your own folk, that's what I always say. My daughter, she's married to a baker up there and they've got two lovely children, you wouldn't see the beat of them anywhere. I've got presents for them in the case up there. My son now, he doesn't like the city—he likes the country. But my husband, you wouldn't get him out of Glasgow. Born and bred there, as you might say. He wouldn't come with me, says he's got the sciatica. But he was worried about me for a while there. It was touch and go, that operation. But I'm all right now. See, if someone was suffering like that and said to me: 'Should I take that operation?' I'd say 'yes' any time. What's the use of living in a chair?"

Lorna must have missed those luxuries, those careless days of lying in the sun on a deck chair, or perhaps, if she had been willing to surrender the disorientation of new frontiers, new parties, new hotels, the shifting orphanage of her travels since clearly her parents were always elsewhere, then she might have expected him to give more than he had done as compensation for that surrender. Whole areas of her conversation were curiously empty as if she knew nothing of ordinary things, as if her knowledge were of other countries, different schools— she had been to so many—horses, nannies and so on.

"What did I do to you, Lorna?" he thought with agony, listening again to the little woman in order to muffle that terrible inner voice.

The woman's words turned interminably in time with the train's wheels. "Of course what can you expect in Castlemilk? But I don't like the way respectable people look at you. There are good people in Castlemilk too. But, as I was saying, they've organised this party especially for me. I'm sure it will go well. Say what you like though, the Glasgow people are warm-hearted. My neighbour (Mrs. Mason I was telling you about) made the dinner for Jack every day, Jack's my husband, my son goes to the canteen. Now, wasn't that nice of her? It's not everybody would do that. But, as I always say, a good neighbour is worth her weight in gold. And Mrs. Mason has never said an unkind word about me, I know that for a fact. But I'll never forget her face, the day I went for my operation. She thought I was going to die. And the day I came home I danced a waltz with her. What a sight we were, her with flour all over her, she does a lot of baking, you see. Nothing from the shops for Mrs. Mason."

The little woman laughed merrily and her laughter was like a bell that one might hear tinkling on a Christmas tree. And Mark remembered:

"The door bell rang twice the week before Lorna . . . and I went to the door and there was no-one there. If I had been superstitious . . ."

Sometimes, before, he had heard the bell in the night but this was in the early evening around eight o'clock and Guy Fawkes Night and Hallowe'en were past. Lorna had thought it might be some pranksters but he had rushed out quickly the second time and he had heard no sound of retreating feet.

He leaned his cheek against the cold glass of the window pane and saw slag heaps, foundries, tall chimneys, wheeling past under a red industrial sky. On a pitch not far from the railway he saw some boys—in striped green and white jerseys and white shorts—playing football. The air seemed absolutely motionless, the cold zero reducing reality to a painting. He felt no hunger: he felt nothing, exactly as one is when anaesthetised by the dentist and it is only much later that one feels the pain and the red gash where the tooth was. His eyes noted objects but asked for no reasons. The little woman had raised her feet to the seat opposite and had gone to sleep as the train rolled on. The lines in her face suggested suffering, a piece of paper that had been creased. As he looked at the face it suddenly smoothed itself out and he saw it as one might see the face on a Roman coin, aloof and cold and serene.

So the train rolled on northwards passing a landscape ever more and more bleak. Sometimes they passed by the sea, looking down sheer cliffs and across at limitless cold waters where seagulls circled in enormous spaces. Here and there a lighthouse could be seen and here and there small villages.

When they were preparing to leave the carriage—after reaching their destination—the little woman said:

"Come and see us if you've got time. The address is 36 Claremont Street. You'll remember it won't you? Excuse me for mentioning it."

Then she was off briskly looking for her son and daughter in law. "36 Claremont Street, 36 Claremont" he repeated to himself as he passed the bookstall and emerged into the air. This was the echoing station at which he had arrived twenty-five years before, at the age of seventeen, having travelled by slow train from bare land to rich, from ragged croft to geometrical farm, seeing from the window in the autumn light here and there a red tractor moving across rich black loam. It was a rich wide land with carefully constructed mathematical farms very different from the stony land from which he had come. There was a feeling of space and fertility, a lack of constriction and yet at the same time a knowledge of boundaries. Man had really conquered this land, man was making use of it for himself. There was no sign of the sea, only the rich inner spaces of a country, controlled and directed, very different from the scattered stony landscape which had been his and which had entered his heart.

Walking out of the station as he had done so long ago he paused to see the beggar sitting there with the black glasses and the cap containing its few pennies. But there was no beggar there now. He halted for a moment at the exact spot seeing himself at seventeen shaken to the core by the unintelligible enormity of beggary, by the blind vulnerable man who threw himself on the mercy of the world. To give him a coin was in some way to become a part of the system which perpetuated his poverty, not to give him one—conceding that he was truly blind and not pretending to be—was to become one of the proud ones, encased in a pitiless hauteur. He stood there, conscience-torn, and eventually walked away too ashamed to, after all, be charitable. Now he felt a certain pity for the embarrassed seventeen year old, emerged into the huge light of the city, standing there perplexed and moving on towards the future which was what he had become.

Where could he go now? To a hotel or back to his old digs?

43

A hotel would be better, because of its anonymity; he could visit the old digs later. So he flagged a taxi and was deposited at a hotel—all hotels had become much the same to him, boxes in which he could leave his case, boxes which could allow him a little freedom—and he left his case in one and walked and walked till he came—quite without intention it seemed—to the university which he had once attended. He looked at it—ivy clad in the falling darkness—imagining, posted on green baize, the results of distant examinations, and smelling the smell of new varnish on stairways. There had been that girl with mauve lipstick whom he had once seen outside the door of the History lecture room—and the History lecturer himself, precise and cold, reading his notes for the fiftieth time defending Mary Queen of Scots. He remembered sitting in the library reading his Donne while the tall woman with the ladder scaled the walls looking for a book for a customer. Images of various kinds and of differing clarity passed before his mind—footballers on the green field, rounders in the sun, sitting shirt sleeved in a lecture room while the green leaves rustled faintly against the windows.

Now there were some cold lights in the university, and beyond stretched the green playing fields flat as billiard tables and more shining, more lush.

Straight up the road, now drizzly and dark, he could see the very place down which he had walked once, years before, shouting to the crisp March air the lines from *Othello*:

"Put up your bright swords or the dew will rust them"

How could one recall the pristine freshness of those days, when literature seemed consonant with life and lines of poetry harmonised with the very light itself?

There was the American student just out of the war—one of the many the American Command had shunted into university till they could organise an orderly demobilisation—a fan of Emerson's with whom he had toured the city and the country-side taking photographs of old buildings, quarries, aerodromes, fields full of summer flowers and salted by the sea

44

air. To him, after all those months, he had offered a book on Transcendentalism which had cost him a great deal of money; stiff lipped, the American looking at him strangely as if he had expected nothing. But he himself could not accept that free expenditure—those weeks, for instance, watching Gilbert and Sullivan in the plush theatre—without guilt. He remembered seeing him off on the train, uniformed in that fine almost silken American cloth. He had never found it easy to part from people and in that sense had been more like the crouching stone than the sparkling stream which moves from point to point without memory or desire.

Looking back it seemed a world without responsibility, a world of poetry, a world unpenetrated by cares from outside itself. Arguments in that cafe in summer or at the back of it, under the green trees, sitting at yellow marble-topped tables while the cafe owner, a parrot who had picked up snatches of cultural information from the students, would shoot out quotations from Camus or Sartre.

Looking back it was an effortless unquestioning passing of examinations watching other students—Medicals and Engineering—slaving all night over their thick pointless books which had neither poetry nor illumination, only information.

Looking back it was a kind of wit, an expectancy that the world would be like that of literature, golden and beautiful.

Looking back he could find nothing there but books, girls briefly met and quickly parted from, lecturers orating on Anglo Saxon and one boy in particular who had turned up, glanced at the paper and had then walked out after writing only his name and a spoof translation of an incomprehensible section from jagged and wiry *Beowulf*.

Looking back it was distant, beautiful and useless. He could not find himself standing there in the cold drizzle. All he could remember was sitting white-flannelled in the park in the heat of summer eating ice cream while the neanderthal-browed Jimmy—now in computers and married with three children—and the slow Fred listened to his butterfly witticisms.

It was a city of stone and light where, confined to his own

45

circle, he had been protected from all that had not been transmuted into art and poetry. Wide eyed he had walked through it yet at the same time as if in a dream, walking the blue bridges at night, going to performances of Gilbert and Sullivan, sitting in poky cinemas where at one time one could buy a seat for an empty jam jar (lemon curd for the balcony?). It was a time of answering questions on Hume, Milton, Horace, Beowulf.

Uneasily he looked about him at the slums in which the university was set, shuddering in the snow, a visitant from another planet, watching two students in long hair with books under their arms striding towards the bus stop, as far removed from him as Martians.

What could he find in this place? Himself? Penetrated through and through by self disgust he waited as for some saviour, as if out of the library directly ahead of him there should emerge a figure who might tell him that his life had not been wasted, that art and poetry were in fact still present even in the middle of this desperate winter, that the lighted windows were sending out meaningful signals into the darkening evening.

That book he had worked on . . . that era with Lorna. He shuddered again, invested by sickness, climbed by ladders of pain.

A fat woman was standing beside him waiting for the bus, weighed down by parcels. For a moment he thought of the other woman, the one on the train, his Leech Gatherer: and even as he stood there he was thinking also of a poem he had once read by Seferis in which the latter had written of revisiting a place in which he had once lived and how his feet sank in the earth, and not only that but he was comparing it mentally with another poem by Lowell on the same theme. He saw only quotations around him everywhere, not a reality but a manuscript, a literary grid, with poems winking on and off.

When he was on the bus a man who spoke with an Irish accent boarded it and tried clumsily to embrace the conductress, a confidant looking girl with blonde hair and a mini-skirted uniform. He slumped down on the seat and took out a wad of

46

pound notes which he sprayed all round him like cards, some landing on the floor, he all the while regarding them owlishly.

"A pound if you'll talk to me," he pleaded whiningly with the peroxided conductress aloofly waiting for his fare. "There you are now, a quid if you'll talk to me." The passengers turned their wintry faces on him and then turned away. The Irishman tried vaguely to retrieve the pound notes but in the middle of his effort fell into a drunken stupor leaving two or three lying on the floor among the bags, with the Christmas parcels and the groceries. Soon he began to snore though from time to time the vibration of his lips shaped the words, "If you'll talk to me."

Mark heard himself saying again to the American: "I bought you this," and the American saying, "I didn't reckon on your . . . ." and had then looked at the stiff honourable face and said: "Thanks a million. Just what I wanted."

But the gifts had been diminished just the same and the American—affluent, outgoing and free—had looked a little saddened like one coming across a stiff necked aristocrat in a disintegrating castle where only the pictures speak of a rich past.

(3)

Roman-nosed, a Caesarian slab, she stared at him from the open door. She doesn't even remember me, he thought with resignation and a certain melancholy. And indeed standing there, compact and squat, assured of her own house, owner of it, with its large bow windows and its rather Victorian furniture and its lodgers bringing in six pounds a week or so each, she represented to him one of the unconscious ones who nevertheless make their way in the world since it never enters their heads that people like them should not do so, and that doing so is a laudable aim.

"Don't you remember me?" he said at last. "Mark Simmons."

47

Her expression which had been suspicious—would she after all now accept him as a lodger in his large brown coat and rather deranged scarf?—changed immediately to one of surprised recognition and effusiveness and he found himself being ushered through the hall into the deserted lounge which a tall long-haired boy left immediately without saying a word. She lit the one barred electric fire (the other bar not being usable).

"That's David," she said, "do you remember David?" And he did remember him as a baby, thumb in mouth, standing in the lobby accompanied by a large white dog which duplicated his own large whiteness. He had never spoken to him or made much of him.

"And what are you doing now?" she said, her small sharp sly eyes scanning him rapidly and halting for a moment at the bulging coat pockets, perhaps—he realised for the first time—thinking that they concealed a present such as a bottle of whisky for Christmas. He cursed himself for forgetting that it was Christmas-time.

"Oh nothing much. I lecture." He nearly said, "I have lectured," but decided against it in the split moment that it took him to see her prosperous-looking thin grey jumper with the string of pearls at the throat. She was not the sort of woman to praise posthumous things.

"A lecturer. Fancy that now. But you'll like a cup of tea, I'm sure." And so later they reminisced for she could afford the time, it being the calm before the lodgers came home for their meal.

"Do you keep in touch with your old friends," she asked.

"You mean Fred and Hugh. No, I've lost touch with them though I heard Fred was now a doctor somewhere."

"Oh yes," she said, "He's that. He's got a lovely family too. They were here last summer travelling in a big blue car. His wife is English, you see, and he was showing her the place. He even took her out to the university. He was the one who was always coming in for the coal, I told his wife." She spoke with a hint of malice as if he had done something illegal. He

48

himself had never confronted her, coward that he was: but then again she had nursed him that time he was ill, hearing from his bedroom in a smell of oranges the hoover humming deep below.

"Who's for the North Pole?" Fred would say, looking up from his medical books. He was a squat dark sort of person, solid of speech and solid of behaviour, though after examinations he was liable to go out on boozing expeditions which took him from one end of the city to the other.

Mark still kept the photograph of the three of them sitting on the lawn beside the house, all in white—white open-necked shirts and flannels, all except Fred who wore a utilitarian brown suit striped like a wasp. Looking at the photograph now, Mark thought that he himself looked rather ghost-like in the bright sun, as if he were either receding from reality or were entering it from some other world.

"And I suppose you're married yourself?" she pursued, seeming perplexed by something about him which she could not define.

"I was," he said briefly, letting her think what she liked.

She paused briefly and then plunged on. "I still have the students though you wouldn't believe what they get up to. They would be taking drugs if it wasn't for me taking a firm hand. And their hair. You've never seen the like of it. They're like girls. I swear you can't tell the girls from the boys. One of them—would you believe it?—put a photograph of some heathen on his bedroom wall. I soon told him to pull that down. I think they're all Communists."

Mark remembered the long discussions he and the other two would have late at night while Edmundo Ros was playing on the radio, obscure philosophical discussions about perennial matters such as Bertrand Russell and his pennies, continuing their debate in their huge beds upstairs (the three of them slept in the one room) while the moon shone in through the window on the ghostly bedclothes.

"You were good at paying for your lodgings," she said. "I must give you credit for that. Not like some of them. Do you remember Miss White? She's a supervisor now." Supervisor of what? he wondered. He had a vague memory of someone eternally knitting like that woman in Anouilh's *Antigone* who had knitted all through the play and then got up at the end, having finished the row, and gone and hanged herself. Not that Miss White would do that. She was a dapper thirty-five year old in blue who was always picking the bones from kippers.

"Did you know Harry had passed away?" she said. Harry was her husband, a vociferous taxi driver keen on football. She dabbed at her left eye delicately with a handkerchief which mysteriously appeared from somewhere. As a matter of fact she had been rather rough with Harry, as he remembered, for Harry wasn't ambitious and kept pigeons which she didn't like. "He came home one night and died in that very chair you're sitting in. Sudden it was. I was making the tea at the time. You mind he was keen on football?"

That had been a major part of his exiguous life, the thin man with the phantasmal moustache who was often to be seen trimming the hedges on a Sunday afternoon.

She talked on and on and he said, "I'm sorry. You were saying?"

"I was saying about the burn on the sideboard. It was Hugh who did that. Only he wouldn't admit it. He's in charge of a factory now in Yorkshire. I get a card from him every year at Christmas. He's married down there with two children, a boy and a girl. Imagine poor Hugh. But he was a devil too. But you were the quietest of them. Fancy seeing you again. Do you remember the night Mr. Black smashed the car up? My, the police were busy that night. And you wouldn't believe butter would melt in his mouth. Him a bank manager and going off climbing mountains every weekend. He was always singing the *Messiah*, do you remember? He was a good singer, he had a good voice. But you never did anything like that. You were a great one for studying. It was a pleasure to hear you talk. I often used to say to myself, 'That boy will be a professor yet.' But do you remember the day you and Mr. Silver had that bottle of port in the lounge (he was in the Customs, you mind) and when I came in Mr. Silver stood up and he said:

"Madam I'll set the table. Madam, I am quite capable of setting the table." That was the only time he ever called me Madam, when he was drunk. I used to remind him of it. And, to top it all, he fell to the floor," she said, still watching Mark carefully.

"Yes, I remember Mr. Silver and Mr. Black." Mr. Black was the one who would play the piano singing "All we like sheep," the light glistening from his bald confident head.

Their exchanges were beginning to lose energy now as if each was casting about for something to say. I was here once, he thought. I sat on this chair and yet it bears no stigmata. Who was it who was here? Was it me or a phantom of myself? It was strange and slightly frightening to think about it but at least his ex-landlady was solid enough, a stone in the flux.

"Will you stay for tea?" she said carelessly as if she didn't really want him to stay and adding almost immediately, "but I expect you'll have lots to do."

"No, thanks, I shall have to be going. I just called for a minute." She did not remark on the oddness of his calling out of the blue at that time of year. She got up (as if she had decided something about him) and so did he. She would certainly have kept Fred and Hugh and their large families and their medical talk and their factory conversation. She was nothing if not normal.

"How very ordinary she is," he thought. "Not at all the person I remember." There was an indefinable air of ageing about her. He looked around him. The furniture imposed itself on him with an almost intolerable weight. He had often looked into that mirror there. Where did reflections go? Berkeley would know, as if it mattered.

"Miss White is married now," she said. "She's in Wales. But all the wives work now even though their husbands may have good jobs. She was a clever woman. I never thought she would marry, though she could knit well."

As they were going out they passed the long haired David again.

"This is the Mr. Simmons of whom I told you so much," said his mother rather obsequiously.

"Congratulations," said the boy, brutally giving him one brief careless look before making his way upstairs. "Bastard," said Mark under his breath but realising that he himself at the same age had been negligent and intolerant as well, brutal in argument and concerned only with that. He noticed it was still the same carpet on the stairs.

"It was so good of you to come," she said standing at the door. He mumbled something and made his way up the road. There had once been a small library there. He remembered entering one evening to see standing on top of a ladder a young girl in black showing fine long legs in the light which poured over the books. He remembered also another girl he had once met in a library, and taking her home one winter's night and kissing her in the doorway. Her face was blue in the light. And finally he remembered another girl he had met on Christmas Day and seeing her home to a brutal slum where he had spent two hours with her mother playing Monopoly. Her mother had been mountainous and smelt abominably. The daughter was brutal in her language and mercenary in her ideas. He remembered her as pale and bitter. He passed the place where the library had been but now there was a radio shop. How terrible it was to feel an anachronism. A city made of silver yielded nothing to his digging. He had left no mark. Some negligence had irretrievably gone.

(4)

As he walked along he stopped at a cafe opposite the town library and gazed at it as if some memory were struggling to emerge from the deep darkness in his mind. He saw himself ascending the steps to the library, then the stairs, past the white statuary on the landing and finally entering the library itself, where he would sit at a table with a miscellany of books around him. Donald was sitting with him at the table, large solid Donald, his Horatio as he often considered him in his princely imagination, Donald who was studying Engineering in his slow amiable way. They would read for some time and at eight leave the room, cross the street and enter the cafe outside which he was now standing. There was a young waitress there at that time—in a cream uniform with a touch of red at the breast—with whom he fancied he was in love though he had never actually spoken to her except to ask for coffee. But there seemed to be an affair of eyes between them which encouraged him and allowed him to leave a possible assignation to a pleasurable future. She would have left school at fifteen, he thought, and the alliance of the educated with the uneducated fascinated him. On one particular occasion he found himself sitting at a corner table with Donald, and Alex who had mysteriously appeared. It was a fine summer evening and he could see through the window with a certain distaste and ennui the statue of Sir Walter Scott looking benevolent and profound in white stone, which however in places was turning a rather plaguey green.

A sin those days everything turned to intellectual discussion; they began—or rather he began—to talk about the tragic hero in Shakespeare; looking back he thought of his university career as a series of conversations picked up, dropped, continued in cafes, on buses, on trams, in lounges and bedrooms. He was maintaining the not unusual argument that the tragic hero was above all a failure.

"In what way would you say a failure?" said Alex falling in with his mood as he so often did: Alex was a classicist, devoted to the enigmas of grammar and philology but he liked to "expand his knowledge".

"He is a failure because he has not entered the world of power and is continually surprised by what he calls evil." They were interrupted at that point by the girl who stacked the dirty cups on a tray and substituted clean ones. In her cream dress she looked like a nurse in a hospital and the curve of her back

53

as she bent over the table was infinitely attractive and pathetic and feminine. He noticed with some curiosity that her hands were trembling and that her voice faltered for a moment when she took their order.

"If he weren't a failure," he went on later, chewing a Blue Riband, "he would have studied what goes on in the actual world. The world of nature doesn't consider itself a failure. The leaf does not pass judgment on itself. That is why I can't understand why Hamlet is considered intelligent."

"But surely," said Donald, "this is one of the main things about Hamlet. I thought Maxwell said that when we were doing the play at school. I'm sure he did. He was supposed to be more intelligent than the people round him. Isn't that why he was so much alone?"

"Yes, I know Maxwell said that. But there is always a reason why people are alone and act like hermits. And the reason is usually not a romantic one, though people insist on making it so. But in what way is he intelligent? What does he use his intelligence for?" He raised his voice so that the girl, bringing the coffees, might hear him though he was quite sure that she wouldn't understand, having, he was certain, left school at fifteen.

"Intelligence is a method that allows us to survive, isn't it? Well, he didn't, did he? When he was confronted by a choice he did not make the right one or rather he didn't do anything at all. And why not? The world of nature can't exist without making choices. Not to make choices is to refuse to live. Hamlet is really a dead man. From the very beginning he is dead."

"Wait a minute," said Donald, "you're going a bit fast, aren't you? The fact that he doesn't survive doesn't mean that he's unintelligent. I mean . . ." He looked genuinely puzzled as if he wasn't quite sure of what to say next and Mark felt again the familiar sense of power in the workings of his own mind.

"Couldn't an intelligent man be run over by a bus?" said Alex, while trails of coffee spume ran down his distinguished chin.

"If he was intelligent he oughtn't to have been. In any case, that is not the point . . ."

"Before you go any further," said Donald ruminatively, "I have a feeling Claudius didn't survive either. Does that make him stupid?"

"Yes, he too was stupid. But, in any case as I said, you're missing the point. People say that Hamlet was intelligent because he nattered on about philosophical matters in an amateurish way and because he found himself full of ennui in the small prison of Denmark. Let me ask you a question then. Why didn't he inherit the throne? And why did the bourgeois Claudius inherit it? Clearly because Hamlet wasn't fit for it."

"Well, you're an English scholar," said Alex tolerantly. "After all I'm only a Latin scholar but there may have been a law stating that the brother . . ."

The girl who was now attending to a woman at the next table looked as if she had just been crying and for a moment Mark nearly put his hand on her delicate wrist as if to comfort her. But the moment passed and it was Donald who handed her the milk jug from their own table, the one next to them being apparently milkless.

"I doubt it," continued Mark after a while, forgetting about the girl, "after all, Rosencrantz and Guildenstern assumed in their conversation with him that he should have inherited. As for what Fortinbras says at the end of the play, that Hamlet would have made a good king had he lived, that's a lot of waffle. How could a man like that be a good king? He turned reflectively on the world around him. Nature goes on, he went inwards. By passing judgment on the world he no longer proved to be part of it. Anyway, animals don't commit suicide and he wanted to, only he was too frightened and spiritual to do even that. He knew nothing about people because he was always thinking about himself. The ruined liberal, if there ever was one. Think of what he did to Ophelia. No, everything he touched turned to lead."

He hoped that the girl had heard that and saw her standing beside an older waitress in the attitude of one who is being talked at in a quiet urgent but hectoring way. He continued rapidly: "He found himself incapable of dealing with the reality around him. He showed no tenderness to Ophelia. Let us admit that he had a certain gift with words but Cervantes is supposed to have had a low I.Q. Creativity doesn't necessarily mean intelligence."

"But surely," said Donald spooning his coffee in a desultory manner, "sensitivity and intelligence are allied. An alarm clock is less easily destroyed than a wristwatch."

"Touché," said Mark admiringly. "That seems right but on the other hand I can't see any obvious connection between sensitivity and intelligence. Hamlet acted incompetently throughout. He didn't weigh the facts up properly. Look at all the people who were killed at the end. He lost control of himself often and acted like a child. He was immature. Conduct which would be inexcusable in others is forgiven in him. Why? I'll tell you why. It's because the scholars have a vested interest in approving of him since he was a scholar himself. What would General Montgomery say about him? Or Patton?" He burst out laughing when he said this.

"Well what about Macbeth then?" said Alex suddenly.

"Touché again. You mean the alliance of sensitivity and brutality. Yes, a bit like Lawrence of Arabia perhaps, or wouldn't you say?"

The girl was now alone in the corner pulling absently at her apron. Perhaps I should ask her out, Mark thought idly. Sometime.

"His treatment of Ophelia was inexcusable," he continued. "No, once for all, intelligence is a faculty which allows us to deal competently with reality. Hamlet didn't have that faculty. Fortinbras had it. Hamlet made blunder after blunder killing Polonius and his student friends who were far less guilty than Claudius. The man was a walking plague. He was responsible for more deaths than even Claudius was and yet we say, 'Oh, but he was so very intelligent'." As Mark talked, range upon range of mountains opened in front of him and then a desert through which he walked, drunkenly talking.

"The fact is that he had a highly developed consciousness which was hostile to life. Why else was he always talking about death? Claudius was right. One should accept death. He couldn't do so. This is not a fact to be admired. Nature goes forward, he was going backwards. His mind was reflecting backwards."

"But why should we accept nature?" said Donald. "If we were to accept nature we wouldn't invent anything to cure people of diseases."

"Exactly. We shouldn't."

"I never knew you were a Christian Scientist," said Alex wryly. Alex was the kind of person who wore a university tie and a university scarf, a clean living, clean limbed boy, who wrote notes very neatly in his exercise book. "In any case," he continued, "all you're saying is applicable to all men of thought. Do you rate Montgomery higher than Mozart?"

"Yes, I do," said Mark defiantly. "I do."

"In that case," said Alex seriously, "there's nothing more to be said, is there?"

"You see," continued Mark in an excited voice as if he were a politician putting forward a manifesto whose contents ought to be acceptable to all right thinking constituents, "ordinary people think that intelligent people are bookish people. But books don't exist in nature. I maintain that if you can't deal with reality then you are a stupid man. That is why Hamlet was stupid. Why did he keep everything to himself? Why was he so excessive? And then he took himself so seriously, thinking that he was the centre of the universe and that his melancholy was a fact of the world and that everybody else ought to be the same. I like to think of Fortinbras striding in there and letting in the sun and enjoying himself. He was the cool man, he had no objection to inheriting the throne. And he probably didn't work after five o'clock. After all life should be enjoyed too."

"Stalin had no objection to inheriting the throne either," said Alex.

Mark continued as if he hadn't heard the interruption. "And

he spent his time mocking an old man who was trying to do his best. What sort of behaviour is that? Yet we approve it. Those scholars approve of it in fiction though they wouldn't approve of their students doing that to them. And he threw away the love of a girl who was sincere and who loved him. There was a streak of cruelty in him, you know. No, you can keep Hamlet as far as I'm concerned." He got up from the stained table, feeling, as it were, an invisible cloak around his shoulders, and himself in the centre of a clear pearly light.

When they were going he noticed that the girl was furtively wiping her eyes. He half stopped again as if there was something he might say to her. But he couldn't think of anything—anything, that is, humanly comforting—though the hands now folded in front of her were white with the effort of keeping them from trembling.

Out again, he felt the air around him as apt for a prince, his head danced with as many thoughts as the stars, with a dry autumnal power, and he felt himself not a Hamlet but a Fortinbras able to hold the world like an apple in his hand; so much so that as he saw the people in their white gloves coming out of the theatre opposite he felt that he should call them back in and put on for them a performance such as they had never seen in their lives before. But they were already chatting with each other—the women in their long gowns and furs, and the men with their white scarves and top hats and tails—and they all looked so contented that he felt that they would not be able to listen to anything he might say.

Soon he had forgotten the girl and was never in fact to see her again, for she disappeared from the cafe as if she had never been. Once or twice he thought he might ask what had happened to her but he couldn't bring himself to do so.

In any case she had no real place in his poetic and intellectual world. She lived in a world of tables and dishes and he could not imagine what that might be like, though he sometimes thought of it and had a hankering for it as Hamlet himself had a hankering for violence and skulls and an ennui which bred such desires. Donald and Alex on the other hand were normal enough to follow without question the route they had got on to, career, children and marriage. He half despised them for this. He couldn't understand why they never seemed to feel the irrevocable absence which he himself felt so that some- times he would stop and wonder why he was in a particular place rather than another and at other times, especially in the evening, his mind was transformed by a radiance as if from another world, so that this world became like a glass of water through which he could see quite tranquilly and in an elated way to the other side. The girl in the cafe however didn't appear in that otherworldly place any more than probably Ophelia appeared in the mind of Hamlet when he was clair- voyant and clear. At moments like these he felt great love for his Horatios, Donald and Alex, who were such three-dimen- sional beings in this world.

(5)

He wandered about all the following day, going into pubs and meeting no-one, eating now and again, now and again staring vacantly at a newspaper. Around five he found himself in the draughty Art Gallery staring at a picture by Paul Klee which showed boats which might have been triangles or triangles which might have been boats and a purple moon and various reddish lights. Its drifting precision—its combination of geometry and play—satisfied his eyes and as he looked at it he felt that this was perhaps how life might be, playful and con- trolled, colourful and disciplined. There was no-one in the gallery but himself and a large bearded student in a duffle coat and, as he sat there, he snuggled into his own coat shivering now and again and feeling that disorientation which racked him. Lorna painted but did paintings of people never of abstractions: there was, for instance, that one which she had done of the hermit, sitting upright against a chair rather like a Graham Sutherland. He had quite liked her work though he had never admitted to doing so: there was another one for instance of a black nun set against a red sunset background, showing an explicit simplicity of the contrasting two colours. He wondered if she would have liked the Klee, studying it as if it contained some secret that might eventually be made known to him. Were these shapes boats or merely geometrical shapes? Were they meant to be on a sea or in space? And was that purple circle really a moon? After a while he wanted to leave but he didn't know where to go. He was tired of drinking rum in pubs and tea in draughty cafes. Then the thought came to him that he might go to that address after all. 32 something street. For a dreadful second he thought that he wouldn't remember it and then he knew that he wanted to go. 32 . . . no, 36 Claremont Street. He would take a bottle of whisky and a cake or something. After all it was Christmas-time. And a taxi.

He went out into the drifting snow and bought a bottle of whisky at a supermarket, and a cake. The assistant had to call him back to give him his change. But eventually everything was all right and he was settled in a taxi taking him out to the place. All the time he was sitting in the taxi he felt impatient and thought he was being cheated as the meter clicked and the taxi man stared deafly ahead. So he gave him only a very small tip, the taxi spraying him with a mixture of snow and water as it accelerated townwards. He found himself in front of a block of tenements of good stone and eventually located No. 36. He paused at the door, the snow falling on his face, and felt he should not go in, but screwed his courage up and rang the bell.

A young moustached man came to the door and stared at him curiously. "Your mother met me on the train and invited me in. I bought these." He shoved the bottle forward and the cake as if they were passports and the man said, "That's all right. Come in." Mark liked the unsurprised matter of fact way he did it, perfectly spontaneously. He entered a smallish room lit with reddish light and containing a Christmas tree. "My mother's out just now," said the young man, "but she won't be long. A neighbour took her out shopping. The name's Harrison. But call me Iain."

"Mark Simmons."

A girl whom Mark thought must be his wife was putting green rollers in her hair in front of a mirror, her arms bare, while a boy and girl were sitting on the floor playing with models of trains and trucks. The girl seemed to be wearing rather large shoes, as if in fact they were her mother's. The room itself was warmed by a coal fire (he himself was more used to electric fires) and decorated with red wallpaper. In one corner of it was a piano, in another a TV set, and there was a bookcase containing some romantic novels and detective stories.

"Sit you down and take your coat off," said Harrison. "This is Mark," he told his wife. "Mark Simmons. He knows my mother."

"She told me to call. I can't stay long," said Mark awkwardly. He felt himself in a very tranquil place and rather ill at ease as if his credentials weren't enough.

"Oh nonsense, you sit down there and I'll get you a drink. Hey, you two, you're in Mr. Simmons' road."

"No, it's all right. Please."

Mrs. Harrison took his coat and he sat down on a chair near the fire. After a while she came back in and sat down on the sofa. Soon afterwards her husband came in with drinks, laying a glass of lager and a glass of whisky beside Mark on a round varnished table.

"Do you take water in your whisky?"

"No, thanks, I prefer it neat. I'm sorry I . . ."

"Nonsense. What are you sorry for? It's Christmas-time, isn't it?"

"Show Mr. Simmons what you got for your Christmas," said Mrs. Harrison. "They're all over the floor with their things," she said apologetically to Mark. "Santa was good to you this year, wasn't he?" she asked the children. "We give them their presents before Christmas Day," she told Mark almost apologetically, "they are so determined."

"Yes," said the little girl with the most entrancing shy sidelong glance at Mark who was holding the lager in his hand and sipping from it.

"What a fine nice place," he was thinking. The bubbles in the lager revolved like miniature snow. Harrison who was sitting opposite him said:

"I work in a baker's shop myself. Perhaps my mother told you."

"Yes and you're always moaning about it," said his wife goodnaturedly. She looked very young, almost schoolgirlish. "He says that he wants to do something scientific. Engineering or something like that. But he's too late now. Sure he is. He's always been good with his hands though."

"Not all that good," said Harrison. "But I can repair watches and radios. It's watching people that does it. You pick it up as you watch them. Bit by bit."

"I don't suppose there's any course you could get," said Mark dreamily. "I mean people go to night school, don't they? Though I must say that I don't know as much about that as I ought to."

"I sent away for a correspondence course once but it was no good. You need to have your Highers. I was quite good at Technical and History when I was in school but I couldn't do English." He threw up his hands in dismay. "I only got twenty once."

"He wasn't interested, that's what it was," said his wife. Mark thought she looked a bright lively girl whose attention however remained with her children through the conversation.

The small boy (who had very fine blond curly hair) came over and leaned on the side of Mark's chair looking up at him. But Mark didn't move. "That's a truck," said the small boy, "and you can bend it like this." He showed how the truck could tip out its contents when necessary. He stood there looking at Mark as if waiting for him to say something: the little girl got up slowly from the floor and went out.

"He got so many presents," said Harrison, "a truck and a tricycle and three games. Show Mr. Simmons the games you got," he said and the boy dashed off. Mark was thinking of what he had heard once about juvenile delinquents: they didn't like touching each other, that was why they used knives. The girl came back in, dressed in a long coat and clopping about in shoes many sizes too large and carrying a small basket. She looked a bit like Little Red Riding Hood.

"Are you going shopping?" said her mother.

"Yes," said the girl shyly.

"And what are you going to buy?"

"A loaf," she began, "cheese . . ."

"And?"

"A tin of sardines."

Her mother swept her up in her arms embracing her fiercely and saying, "You're a caution, a wee comic." The little girl put her head round her mother's embrace and glanced shyly at Mark turning her head away again immediately.

"A wee comic," said the boy coldly. "I've brought my game."

He opened it out on the floor. It was something to do with weapons, murderers and rooms and it worked by a process of elimination. That is to say, one had to find the murderer on the basis of various facts.

"Let's try it," said Harrison. "They bring out so many games I don't know how half of them work."

They spread the paraphernalia out on the floor, Mark reading the instructions aloud. There were three sets of cards, one with names of weapons, one with names of characters, and one with numbers or names of rooms. The game was played with dice and was quite difficult to understand.

"We'll have to find the point of it," said Mark, quite interested though there was a band of pain all round his head. The children were spreadeagled on the floor looking up at him, the husband and wife ensconced above them in chairs.

"I think," said Harrison, "you have to find out who the murderer is and what weapon he used and what room the murder was done in."

"Murderer, murderer," shouted the little boy and the girl looked at him coldly.

They found another set of cards which they could use for elimination purposes. In the centre of the small table they placed a folder which apparently contained the name of murderer, room and weapon: this packet was sealed.

"Ah, I know now," said Mark at last. "We have to eliminate till we find the three things." He felt that he should be able to understand the game instantaneously. Funny, he and Lorna had never played any games. He had once learned chess himself but gave it up because it was too dry. In any case he preferred doing problems rather than playing against an opponent.

The children looked to the game and then back at him and then at the board again.

"The number you throw on the dice takes you to a room," said Mark, sweating. "We'll have to have another look at the rule book." He read the rules out loud, half understanding them as he read. Harrison was looking down at the two children, not saying anything.

"Anyone can shout at any time if he knows the three things. But if he's wrong he can't have another shout," said Mark. "Well," he added judiciously, "that seems clear enough."

"You leave the dice just now till Mr. Simmons is ready," said Harrison, and Mark wondered if the reason why he had brought the game out was to save himself from embarrassed silence. "These games are so complicated now," he said to Mark. "In my day it was just ludo and cards."

"I think we're getting the hang of it," said Mark, feeling the band of pain tightening and taking the tea which Mrs. Harrison held out. He left the piece of cake on the side of the armchair as he was trying to concentrate on the game.

"Eat your cake," said Harrison. "We'll finish the game later." But Mark concentrated on the game, screwing up his forehead.

"Let's start from the beginning again," he said. "Now, the dice. That's the first thing." They all waited obediently.

"You first," he said to the girl. He played the dice for her and moved her piece, representing the suspect.

"That's all right so far," said Mark knitting his brows, determined that he would discover how the game worked. Harrison was smoothing his daughter's hair abstractedly. "And now," said Mark, "it's me next." He moved his piece and handed the dice to Harrison. "Oh, I forgot," he told the girl, "you have to say who murdered whom and in what room." They moved her appropriate piece and he moved his own.

So they played till finally Mark said that he'd got the hang of it now and they put the game away. He leaned back in his chair, drained of energy. The boy and the girl went back to playing with their trucks and Harrison said:

"My mother should be coming soon. Do you want to watch TV?"

"If you want to."

"We'll leave it just now," said Mrs. Harrison. There was a companionable silence during which Mark almost fell asleep. He was astonished at how quickly and unquestioningly he had been accepted and thought how different might have been his own behaviour and attitude if a complete stranger had come to his house. Harrison began to talk of a plane that had just crashed. "I've got a model of that type," he said. And he began to tell Mark a great deal about planes. Later he talked about watches and how British Mean Time was set. He seemed to know a great deal about various things, especially technical ones, and Mark could hardly follow him. Somewhere from the deep past memories were emerging of people he used to know rather like Harrison, practical people, but perhaps not so well up in technicalities. It astonished him how much he had lost touch with them. Later they got on to a discussion about time, and again Mark was amazed at Harrison's perspicacity and when later still they talked about TV he discovered that Harrison's favourite programme was Monty Python's Flying Circus, though his wife didn't like it and considered it to be unintelligible rubbish.

"Sheila thinks it's a lot of old rubbish," said Harrison. "But I think it's pretty funny. Did you see the one about the bored office worker? He was going to his work and this man was shot and he walked over him without looking, carrying his brolly, you know. And he bought cigarettes from a woman at a kiosk and she was in starkers. But this bloke didn't notice." He laughed out loud. "And he came to this bus stop and there was a queue and there was a man with a gun killing everybody, knocking them off, you know. And he was just about to get to him when the bus came and this office worker went on to it. And when he got home his wife said, 'And what sort of day did you have, dear?' And he said, 'Just the usual.' He had a moustache, this fellow, no, I can't remember, I thought he had a moustache. And he had this brolly and he hung it up in the hall." He began to laugh so loudly that he nearly spilt the tea. And all this time Mark couldn't think of anything to say.

"And what about all these silly cartoons?" said his wife.

"I like them. I think they're great. Do you like the programme?" he asked Mark.

Mark said, "Very much", but he found he couldn't remember a single show in any detail.

"There was a radio programme called 'I'm sorry I'll Read That Again'," he said. "That was very good. I don't suppose you listen to the radio much."

"Not much," said Harrison. "Finish your whisky. We got lots of it this year."

At this moment a woman appeared at the door and the children ran over to her.

"Just came in for a minute," she said with a quick glance at Mark. "Don't get up. My husband is taking me out. We're going to the White Hart for a drink."

"Well, well, look at her," said Harrison. "All in furs. Who left you these?"

"I bought them, cheeky. And how's Santa been treating you?" she asked the children. They told all the things they had got and she listened with great and generous interest.

"Isn't that good?" she said. "Make sure you don't break your neck with the tricycle," she told the boy. Her furs weren't really very good and didn't look expensive and they didn't suit her very well since she was rather short and she didn't wear the correct sort of stockings and shoes with them.

"Oh, he won't break his neck. He's got it screwed on all right. He got plasticine from the lady opposite. He's always over there. He's looking out for himself," said Harrison.

"Well, make sure that you make a model for me," said the woman. The child flushed with pleasure and Mark was amazed at how exactly and rightly she spoke, saying naturally the proper thing that the boy wanted to hear, though at the same time she looked, as far as style went, rather vulgar. She took a mirror out of her handbag and studied her face briefly.

"One of these days you won't see anything in the mirror," said Harrison, who seemed to have got into the habit of teasing her.

"Listen to him." She waved him away. "And I'd better be getting back. My husband's trying to fasten his braces."

She glanced again briefly at Mark before leaving and he knew that later on she would want to know everything about him and this annoyed him.

No sooner had she gone than a young boy and girl came in, the boy with a bottle of gin which he began to pour out for everyone. The girl wore a short yellow skirt and had a fixed smile on her face which probably came from shyness. The boy was long and lanky and rather silent.

"We're going to a dance," the girl explained. "If we ever get there. He's been stopping at every close on the street for the past hour. We started off at seven and now it's eight o'clock."

"Good old Shuffling Dick," said Harrison. "When did you give up the whisky?"

"Him! He likes gin better."

"It's all that dust from the quarry," said Harrison.

"I started on it after I got merrit," said the boy ducking away from the girl who was about to hit him playfully.

"Ay, he was proper thin then but he gets fed nowadays. Look at his waist."

"Porridge, I bet," said Harrison. "That's a new one. Porridge and gin. That's better than Andy Stewart." The girl passed a glass with some gin to Mark, who sat in his chair not knowing what to say, and envying them their free uncomplicated talk.

"Still working at the quarry?" said Harrison.

"Ay, but not much longer."

67

"He's been saying that for years," said his wife.

"You'll get your pension from there, yet," said Harrison.

"And you'll get it from the baker's," said his wife. "He's been saying he's going to move from there for years," she told the girl. "But he'll never move. He's too frightened."

"Frightened. Listen. If you say that again I'll tan your backside." And so the conversation went on. It turned out that the young boy was very interested in weapons and was building up a collection of them. He was very enthusiastic and told Harrison about his collection which included an Iron Cross, a bayonet, and a Luftwaffe badge.

"You're a proper Nazi," said Harrison. "I bet you've got a whip as well."

"Not yet," said the youth's wife, "but he's been saying he's going to get one."

"You're like Monty Python," said Harrison, "beating your wife in the Council house with a Nazi whip."

Finally the girl got up saying, "Listen, if we're going to get to that dance we'll have to move. Come on." And she dragged him off the sofa. All this time Mark listened, amazed at the apparently unworried life that he was watching. He felt profoundly that he had missed something and sensed himself as in some way inferior to these people, who didn't seem to work hard and yet lived well, wore reasonably good clothes, drank and ate well. What book had said that their lives were constricted? How far he had come from his own origins! Their lives weren't as constricted as his. He felt himself stiff in the chair, like a piece of furniture that had been brought in, all angles, while these people moved around him much more freely, spontaneously, without thinking, though at the same time they could talk about a lot of things. The boy started to talk about the dynamiting in the quarry. "Thank Christ we haven't had any accidents yet," he said, "though if Morrison goes on the way he's going we'll have one."

"All right I'm coming," he said at last, allowing himself to be dragged to the door. The two girls stood talking for a while about restaurants and how many tips waitresses got. Then the boy and the girl left. No sooner had they gone than the mother came in.

"A friend of yours," said Harrison.

"Yes. The gentleman I met on the train. I'm so glad you could come. Oh, my feet. Is there any whisky left?"

"For your feet?" said her son laughing.

"Of course not."

"If you didn't drink so much your feet would be much better. When she had that operation," he told Mark, "they found her veins were full of whisky."

"You shut up. I don't drink anything at all. Except tea and sometimes Ovaltine. It's just the walking, that's all. Look." She got up and executed a neat Highland fling which evoked a burst of cheering and laughter from the others.

"Fighting fit," she said, sitting down again.

"And who's fit?" said her son, pouring out some whisky.

"And how are you liking your holiday?" she asked Mark. "The two of us were talking all the way up on the train," she told her son and daughter-in-law. "It was perishing cold on that train. And the service. I never saw anything like it."

"I was very interested in what you were saying," said Mark more stiffly than he intended.

"I was telling this gentleman all about my ailments," she said. "One thing about that hospital, they were always getting you up when you were just dozing off. But I liked the nurses. They were kind. People can be very kind," she told Mark. "The neighbours were. There was nothing they wouldn't do."

"That's because you look so small and helpless," said her son.

How warm they are, Mark thought. And he wondered if it was all just for his benefit. The son started to tell a story of an old man who lived by himself and went off with a gun every Saturday afternoon. "God knows what he shoots, cows perhaps. But it gives him an interest."

"Ay, that's the thing," said his mother. "Once you lose interest you've had it. I had a cousin once who committed suicide. She never said goodnight when she went to bed and when they went to wake her in the morning she wasn't there. She had drowned herself in a pond. She was only twenty-six." The daughter-in-law told of a story she had read in the paper about an old woman who had got up in the middle of the night and walked out into the snow carrying a hot water bottle. She was eighty-seven years old.

"You've got to watch out for that," said the son. "Little things. If they don't take in the milk or something like that. That's a danger signal."

"I must be going," Mark was thinking. "I can't stay here all night." He saw the mother looking at him and then turning away quickly. He felt naked and vulnerable and stiff. "I don't know anything about people," he said to himself. "I'm like a plague."

"Your shops aren't as good as ours," said the mother to her daughter-in-law. "They're more expensive and the shop assistants aren't so friendly. In Glasgow they call you 'dear'," she explained to Mark. "Why are your shops so expensive?" she asked her son.

"Freight."

"What did you find dearer?" said the daughter.

"I thought all the stuff was dearer," and this led to a long conversation which had to do with bread and curtains.

"Were you buying a diamond bracelet for Sheila?" said Harrison.

"I didn't have my chauffeur with me," said the mother in a mock posh accent. "That's what the queen does, you know. She never carries any money. She's got this man behind her and he carries her purse full of guineas. She pays for everything in guineas. She orders anything she wants and this tall man puts his hand in this bag full of guineas and pays."

So the conversation continued. Mark made no move to go. He didn't want to face his hotel. He did however make one attempt which was shouted down. After that Harrison got on to rockets and nuclear war. It turned out that he was as knowledgeable about rockets as about many other things.

Finally, Mark found himself alone with the mother, at midnight.

"You're very unhappy," she said. "It can't be as bad as that." And for two hours he talked to her in the small warm room, able like the Ancient Mariner to speak at last. He remembered later her small serious face, the whisky he drank, and at last being ushered into a small bedroom from which he rose at seven in the early grey morning illuminating his watch by a match and arriving at his hotel in the cold snowy air after walking all the way.

Part two

(1)

He taught girls in a small college which was where he had met
Lorna, in the middle of introducing them to *The Waste Land*
which they, in their invincible normality, didn't like, complaining that it was all very gloomy, though he himself liked it
enormously, mainly because it allowed one to talk about so
many other things apart from the poetry, such as fertility rites,
(*The Golden Bough*, which he had never really read) and Com-
munism. He had been brought up on poetry where you had
to use your mind and where there was a certain puzzle element
and despised the kind of thing that they on the whole liked,
an undemanding, luscious, vague pop stuff. The girls of course
listened, never dreaming of arguing with him, looked pretty,
took notes and didn't understand a word of the poem, which
he discovered when he had a look at their essays where everything he said was wrongly emphasised and connected, rather
like events in a bad newspaper. He had to learn therefore to be
very simple and repetitive (a thing which he found increasingly
difficult) for these girls weren't at all interested in literature,
only in getting a ticket which would take them out to teach.
Looking at them, so young and fresh and pretty, he vaguely
understood why they didn't like Eliot, though he would put
the thought away from him.

He was quite a good teacher and reasonably witty with a
sort of easy wit which appealed to the girls and which they
understood. His favourite lines from *The Waste Land* were the
ones about the typist and the drying combinations set against
a red romantic sunset. He thought this rather funny and so
did they. He was no authoritarian though at times their
cowishness irritated him, their placidity got on his nerves. He
was happy with literature at the beginning: he didn't believe
that it had anything to do with politics, though, according
to the papers, most university students were followers of the
egregious Che Guevara, and actually had pictures of him on

their bedroom walls. The girls at the training college certainly hadn't heard of him. He himself had never been rebellious in university and was happy to get drunk on Shakespeare's poetry, which would have been considered rather odd nowadays as far as he could understand.

Of course the girls in the college weren't rebellious either. Nor were the teachers. A training college was different from a university. They were all transmitters of an old culture and therefore conservative: it wasn't their job to question things and in any case the pace in the small town was such that protest would appear ridiculous, rather like seeing a man driving along the local street, not a very long one, at a hundred miles an hour.

One day Lorna had impinged on his notice. He was in the middle of talking about the fertility imagery in *The Waste Land* and explaining how the central theme of the poem was fertility and barrenness, including even the sequence in the pub, when an empty milk bottle rolled down the wooden steps on to the floor in front of him. He stared at it in amazement (was the milk after all something to do with fertility imagery?), the book in his hand, and then across the desks to where Lorna in her untidy coat was leaning forward as if preparing to retrieve the bottle, trying not to giggle. Suddenly she made a little rush to the front and then with a queer little bow rushed back to her seat again while all the girls looked at her and then at him. He didn't say anything at all, only she had been brought to his notice.

She wasn't at all what one might call beautiful or even pretty. She had high cheekbones rather like those of a Red Indian and she looked rather untidy and awkward, the sort of person who might very well be carrying milk bottles around and letting them roll down steps in classrooms. But what she did give was an impression of animation a sort of scattered liveliness.

Ever since then he had noticed her more and more. She would come to the front after the class was over and ask him questions about Eliot, for example whether he was married, and where he had got his fertility symbolism from. It was quite clear that not only was her interest in literature minimal, but that she had in many ways the mind of a child. An essay of hers stated that Eliot was keenly interested in Indian religions and that his use of Sanskrit showed a very modern intelligence as did his knowledge of John Donne. Every statement he had made was returned to him like the reflection in a spoon, distorted and fattened and absurd. He had tried to explain this to her but she wouldn't or couldn't understand. She seemed to be implying: Why can't Eliot say what he means straight out, as she did herself?

In the middle of term she went away on holiday and wrote to him from Venice a breathless letter in very large round script. She seemed to have plenty of money—or rather her parents had—and as far as he could understand she had been all over the globe whereas he himself had never left the country. So she had a certain helter-skelter exotic quality which appealed to him, and this breathless negligent air was reproduced in her letters, which were quick and observant. She described beautifully the old woman she had met in Venice with the lorgnette and the canals and the guides. ("You wouldn't have liked the guide, he smelt abominably.") Her glancing exquisite prose, unpunctuated and misspelt, made a great impression on him because of its brightness, its sudden flickering movement and its sheer power of observation. It was full of parentheses and postscripts and was very long as if she had spent a week on it. In fact it was ten pages long and the best part was the one describing the practice life-boat drill with one dowager explaining that she couldn't go into the boat without her maid who happened at the time to be seasick in her cabin. He had received it one morning while mooning over his porridge in Mrs. Walton's lodging. He couldn't help contrasting his own narrow life with the spaciousness of Venice and the gipsyish Lorna with the green faced Mrs. Walton, whose main occupation seemed to be to watch for him when he came in at night. Lorna wrote of champagne and giggling parties and trying to learn Italian and her adventures in the market place, reproducing fragments of Italian like a miraculously gifted bird. She

77

was like one of those bright young things of the thirties because of her carelessness both as to dress and manners among the other dedicated and serious girls who were all wanting to become teachers in primary schools.

He was rather surprised at getting the letter, and immensely flattered too. He was hoping he would get another one (she didn't put an address on the letter) but one day she appeared at the lectures again as if nothing had happened. He found himself more and more inventing witticisms that would please her and thinking of her as distinct from the other members of the class.

As a matter of fact he had been thinking he ought to get married for he was getting rather old now and a bit tired of digs. Mrs. Walton infuriated him not by anything she did but simply because she was there at all. He wanted more freedom and more space. He wanted in theory to be able to lie down on the embroidered bedspread in his dirty shoes. He wanted to come in drunk at three in the morning without running into a strategically placed umbrella stand but knew that this wouldn't be possible for her will was stronger than his and her silences more secure.

The Head of his Department—a man called Wilkinson— had mentioned the idea of marriage to him. Sometimes he would be invited to call at Wilkinson's house and he would arrive there and pull the bell which was attached to a long rope and wait for a bit, casting his eye round the garden and the gravel till Wilkinson loomed against the glass door. Wilkinson had a rather plump wife with crinkling eyes who would listen to her husband talk in his ranging confident mediocre manner as if he were saying things of the greatest importance. He was the kind of man you might start a discussion on evil with only to find at the end that you were talking about a delinquent milkman. All philosophical discussion turned into anecdote under his unremitting bland mind. To argue with him was like playing with an inferior chess player: you lost the game mainly because your opponent did all the wrong things.

Wilkinson would often say things like: "I wonder whatever happened to Shaw. He used to be with me at university. He was a man who got straight A's in his literature but he wouldn't do any Anglo Saxon. The last I heard of him he was teaching English to the Congo mercenaries." And he would shake his head over the wastefulness of brilliance. Or he would say, "I don't think Murray made the right move. He should have applied for that job six years ago." Yet Wilkinson was a man of great sincerity and probity. One knew where one was with him and the answer was nowhere. He had written one book about dress in the Middle Ages but otherwise he had no real passions, only enthusiasms.

At the end of the evening he would show Mark to the gate, their feet crackling on gravel, and he would stand there talking to him and saying that he ought to get married. "People who aren't married aren't taken seriously, you know. I'm saying that for your own good." And Mark would listen and then set off for his digs under the stars, passing on his way a loch with two swans on it, drooping their heads among the reeds. He often wondered how deep the loch was after a conversation with Wilkinson.

One day he came out of the college with some books over his arm. It was a fine sunny day, one of those days which remind people of Paris and the Champs-Elysées or an American campus with young green fluttering trees winking their leaves all around. He didn't know what he was going to do that afternoon or for that matter that evening. As he stood there he heard what sounded like an explosion and there was Lorna driving along in her antiquated car. She stopped and leaned out of the window, her hair blowing slightly in the slight breeze.

"A lift?" she said in her careless rather aristocratic voice. Without hesitation he went forward and entered the car and they drove off past a number of girls who were watching them with interest. But he didn't care, he just wanted to be out of there for a while.

"Where are you going?" he said.

"I thought," she said, "you might come along to my flat and I could offer you a steak. I'm not a great cook but you look half starved most of the time."

It didn't surprise him in the least that she should be as abrupt as this: in fact it was what he would have expected from her.

"You must be tired of those bloody people," she said, careering past a car with a fat man in it who gestured vaguely after her.

"All right," he said. "Only I must buy a half bottle of whisky. I'll have to contribute something."

"If you like but I warn you I won't drink anything."

They got out at a pub to which he sometimes went and he bought a half bottle after which they continued and eventually stopped at a large rambling house with a rambling garden.

"I rent a flat here," she said. "There's no-one but me and the owner who's a perfectly foul person but I never see him except in the morning. He's always repairing engines."

He climbed the steep steps and entered the house: it occurred to him afterwards that in a perfectly typical fashion she had left the door unlocked. He found himself in a room decorated in black and red and sat down on a black leather sofa beside a pile of newspapers among which were the *Observer* and *The Times*. She followed him in and then went into the kitchen. He took out the half bottle and poured some into a glass which he found on a sideboard, shouting to her whether she wanted any.

"No, thanks," her voice came back from the kitchen. "None at all. I've given all that up. I used to drink but there's no point to it."

Beside him he saw an open book by Henry James and wondered whether she had left it there for his benefit: there were also a number of records by people he had never heard of. She came back in while he was thinking about this and curled herself up on the floor in her black tights and black jersey, looking cool and remote, not even wearing lipstick.

As he drank his whisky rather quickly he made small conversation. "How much do they charge you for this?"

"Oh, about seven or eight pounds a week. I don't know. Something like that."

"How do you like it here yourself?" she said.

"Oh, I'd better not say anything about that. I've been here for about twenty years, no, slightly less. That ought to answer your question. Sometimes I like it, sometimes I don't." He was astonished to find himself in the flat at all, and drank more whisky.

"Do you drink a lot?" she said. "My relatives drink a lot. No, that's not quite true. My aunt doesn't. I mean my London aunt. Down south of course it's drugs now. You would be amazed at the kind of lives they lead. The place is rampant with homosexuals. They send each other flowers."

"No," he said, "I don't drink a lot. It's just that tonight I couldn't stand going back to the digs, and that's why I am here. I don't like whisky all that much. It's got an appalling taste. But I shall drink it just the same. I see you're reading Henry James," he added.

"I've only started. I always feel that I ought to read more. But I'm terribly ignorant. In any case I don't like him. He's very slow. He goes on and on about people's souls."

"What do you do when you're not up here? I don't suppose you really want to be a teacher."

"Good God, no. I just thought it might be a good racket for a while. I'm in London most of the time. I meet all sorts of what you would call superficial people, horrible people. Then there are the beautiful girls down there. Models. They take everything off and remake themselves. Some of them are quite lovely. They are like paintings. I feel so ugly beside them. So clumsy."

"Why should you feel like that? You are not at all ugly," and he drank some more whisky.

"Oh but I am. I'm clumsy. I can't help it. I look like a squaw or something. These girls are all tall and blonde and lissom and they haven't got a brain in their heads. What do you do with yourself?"

"Me? Nothing. Nothing at all. When it comes down to it I

81

do nothing at all." He drank some more whisky and the extraordinary thing was that it didn't seem to have any effect on him. And all the while she was kneeling on the floor in her fine black clothes, cool and distant.

"I'm sure you could write a book," she said. "I wish I was talented but I'm not. I have no talent for anything. Don't you think that's terrible? But you can at least talk about Eliot." And she laughed a little. "He sounds an old bore but perhaps he wasn't."

"But you've travelled everywhere," he said.

"Oh yes I have, but I remember nothing of it all. South Africa, Italy, Greece, the lot—you name it, I've been there. And I can't remember a thing about any of these places. Not a thing." She got up suddenly. "I'd better put that steak on and warm it up." She disappeared and he drank more whisky, feeling that he would like to stay in that room all the time, it was so huge and the paintings were so bright, and everything was thrown about so negligently.

After a while she came back and knelt as before on the floor.

"You're not at all ugly," he said. "I don't know where you get that idea from. You're interesting, which is more than can be said for those other cows. It's appalling the way they sit there and feed on stuff they don't at all like. Why don't they have the guts to tell me to go to hell with my T. S. Eliot?"

"As I might do, you mean?"

"Yes. But perhaps that's not fair. You've got money and they haven't, so it's easier for you."

"I wouldn't say it was easier. You don't know much about me. Isn't that sunset lovely?" she said looking out of the window, where indeed there was a technicolour sunset irradiating the sea, among a lot of purple clouds.

"Oh, it's beautiful here," he said carelessly.

"You said that as if you had something against it."

"Not really. Well perhaps it's a bit like the Garden of Eden. One feels the ennui for violence. There's some French expression for it, I think."

"I've seen quite a bit of that, one way or another," she said quietly.

He stared into the burning sunset against which her black clothes stood out clearly, like coal about to be burnt and he said:

"I think perhaps Italy is the place I would most like to visit if I could bring myself to go anywhere."

"It's quite sordid really. People with delusions of grandeur, you know. I didn't like it. I like quiet places. I like this place. I don't know why but I do like it. The people are very kind. I remember one night I went along to a local concert and they were very nice. This woman talked to me all night and invited me to see her. I think I shall go."

"By all means do," he said, drinking some more whisky. Suddenly he leaned forward and kissed her lightly on the lips, which were very chaste and cool like those of a child.

She rose and they went in and ate the steak which was not at all badly cooked though he only vaguely dabbed at it, for he still had the whisky glass in his hand. As a matter of fact he didn't drink all that much but he felt rather nervous. He hadn't met anyone quite like Lorna before and also he had a fine feeling of freedom with her, as though most things people would do didn't surprise her. She was clearly worried about the uselessness of her life. "After all," she said, "I'm twenty-four and I've done nothing." He thought that at times she sounded rather wistful. But she certainly had seen far more than he had ever seen. She had met quite a lot of people whose names were known to him from books and could tell him intimate details about them which she had picked up in random gossip.

"This is what I miss," he said. "You can't do this in my landlady's. Nobody can. Nobody could. When Mrs. Walton says Wednesday was made for mince then God himself couldn't convince her otherwise. She is the triangle of the universe."

Lorna laughed, showing white teeth in a brown gipsyish face and then attacked her steak again. "I'm sorry," she said. "I'm really hungry."

He left his own steak and wandered back into the room they were in before asking, "Who is this reproduction by? The one on the sofa here."

"Bacon," she said through a mouthful of steak. "I bought it recently."

He sat down on the sofa again and drank more whisky.

"You certainly do knock it back," she said half admiringly. "I could never drink like that though I have a cousin who does. He's always being picked up by the police. Bailing him out is getting monotonous."

"Is that true?" he asked.

"Of course. Why not? He's a cruel bastard really." She curled up on the floor again and burst out laughing.

"Why are you laughing?"

"Nothing much. Just wondering what the other girls would think. I suppose they play hockey."

"Just like Wilkinson," he said.

"Who's Wilkinson?"

"Oh, nobody you know. He's an enemy of the spirit."

"And does he play hockey?" she said perfectly seriously.

"You know," he said in a blurred voice, "people are always telling me I ought to get married. They say that people aren't taken seriously unless they are married. It is one answer I suppose."

"Of course it is. My mother is always telling me the same thing."

"Why don't you send out for another half bottle?" he said. "Lift up the phone and tell the local hotel to send a flunkey along with a silver tray."

"I don't need any." She started talking again. "You know, when I was in Venice they knew all about this college, all these purple women. They all called me honey because they couldn't remember my name. And one day we practised life-boat drill. They all staggered along on their crutches. You should have seen the fine young English officers all present and correct and all trying to seduce me. You would probably have known all about the life-boat drill. You're rather clever, I think.

84

My parents go everywhere you know. As long as they give me money they think that I'm no longer their responsibility."

She looked at him gravely and said, "Look, if you're getting pissed, I'll drive you home to Mrs. What's her name and decant you there."

"On the contrary," he said, "we shall not go near Mrs. Walton in my present state. I shall creep back under cover of night. Tell you what, we'll go out somewhere. Let's spend all night drinking. I think I have some of my cheque still left. And in the morning we shall return, as Macarthur said."

"Macarthur? Who's that?"

"A Scotsman. Just like Makarios."

She laughed at that for she had heard of Makarios. "All right then, we'll go out and find a hotel and you can spend the remains of your cheque if that's what you want. But I don't see any reason why you shouldn't stay here."

"No, we won't stay here. For the reason that we've run out of drink. And we'll drive till we find an inn and drink wine and pretend we're in Venice just like Henry James. Did you know that Henry James wrote a story set in Venice, though I can't remember it at the moment. It's about a manuscript, I think. And then we'll gather hyacinths just like that girl in *The Waste Land*, Eliot's hyacinth girl."

"I'd better get my coat then." He swayed a little as he got on to his feet but he didn't feel at all sick, merely blurred in a satisfactory manner.

As they were going out the door Lorna paused looking out at the sunset. "I like this place," she said. "I adore it."

"What?"

"Nothing. I just said, look at these colours. If I could only paint them."

And indeed, even to his blurred vision, the sky with its purplish cinders at the heart of a large expanse of fire was breathtaking in its splendour.

"Another Troy for her to burn," he thought with his aptitude for quotations. Perhaps Helen was rather like that, free and brown and gipsyish and not at all lissom and tall and

85

blonde. A cat ran past them and she bent down and petted it. Its large eyes stared up at them and it purred round her legs. Mark ignored it, negotiating the steps with great care. He felt in fine fettle though his vision was a bit blurred. In fact he preferred the world like that, sometimes. They drove off in the direction of the splendid sunset looking for a pub, or better still a hotel.

(2)

He had been growing discontented with the college for a long time, situated though it was in a small lovely town by the sea, one of those small towns elegantly laid out with trees arching the avenues and middle aged spinsters riding along very upright on bicycles with the messages in baskets in front of them. Their terraced house—his and Lorna's—was a little on the outskirts—not far from a large manorial boarding house which stood on the corner, and also not far from a hospital which was led to by winding gravel paths. The street proliferated with Bed and Breakfast signs that summer, and indeed every summer, and landladies woke to an exciting fresh day of telling their guests which famous spot to visit, what to do during the course of the day, and what the significance of tower or ivied ruin was. Permanent lodgers who had lasted out the winter found themselves in annexes and children fresh out of school were sent off to stay with relatives so that their rooms could be used. Hotel owners and boarding house keepers complained that "this was the worst season ever". No-one could decide whether the visitor wanted a lovely unspoiled place or whether he wanted a miniature version of Blackpool and so there were rows in the Council which were reported reasonably objectively in the local paper. Mark's neighbours, so far as he knew them, were a doctor and his wife who kept themselves to themselves and he was quite pleased about that.

He could not understand why he was growing discontented

but he felt it had something to do with the lack of intellectual content in his life. The girls were pleasant but in the end uninteresting and unenthusiastic. Most of the teachers had been there for a long time and had resigned themselves to staying. He himself had been there for a long time but hadn't resigned himself. Year after year he felt flutterings of departure—especially in late spring and early summer—but hadn't moved. Why hadn't he? At one time, in the beginning, he had found the place, especially in summer, visionary and radiant: it was as if in those early days the leaves of the trees and the leaves of the books duplicated each other or rather were echoes of each other as if literature itself could bring news of spring. In those days he was like a missionary who entered a classroom to bring the gospel to his students. Looking back now he realised that these transformations had been effected by himself, they didn't reside in his students who were ordinary and dull. It was he who had been the alchemist transmuting the lead into gold. The energy had been all his, the radiance had been his.

And his colleagues too in those early days had been like missionaries. Now however he saw them as tired and disappointed people. Wilkinson he began more and more to despise. He was one of those energetic men, tall and thrusting, who have warm handshakes and irremediably mediocre minds. He played golf, a game which Mark thought stupefyingly boring, and unsuited to the intellect which God or evolution had conferred on man.

Mark felt more and more that he was caught inside a web of manoeuvring. These people weren't interested in literature or anything else except how to get the best for themselves. If Shakespeare could be betrayed for a mess of pottage then he would have to take his chances. There was one man—not in the English Department—who was always ordering books for the library and who kept up a running feud with Miss Diamond who was in the English Department and had been assigned the job of librarian. This Maitland—the head of the Geography Department—who had taken an instant and inveterate dislike to her, was coming in day after day with long lists of the most expensive American titles, none of which was in the library but which he was determined would be. He had a flash bristly moustache and talked in the most maddeningly reasonable way which had the effect of almost driving Miss Diamond insane. The Principal of the College was a small man who whenever you met him put his hands on your shoulders and gazed into your eyes saying with great conviction and the most lucid honesty, "My hands are tied." The result was that nothing was ever done and head of departments regarded him with open contempt.

It was not a large college and sometimes Mark regretted that he had not stayed on at University in order to get a Ph.D., for such work might have suited him better, given him more space and scope. The atmosphere was more like that of a school and the girls were in fact very schoolgirlish and unformed in their opinions and attitudes. As they walked about the streets of the town they seemed to sport phantom uniforms and to recall ghostly hockey games.

Many of the lecturers too had become characters. One of them who taught in the Maths Department was famous mainly for his skill in solving the Ximenes crossword and another for his ability to play bridge. Nothing that had been done by anyone was ever forgotten and was likely to be cast up to him years afterwards. For instance, one of them had once gone home in his gown and this story or legend was transmitted from generation to generation. Or if someone had driven a car in the wrong direction round a roundabout then this too was remembered.

At first Mark hadn't noticed these things. He was too busy with his lecturing and also with visiting his girls who delivered their practice lessons in schools in the adjacent city offering their little poems ("The Daffodils" for instance) like bouquets to pupils whose small beady eyes were more concerned with what the girls were wearing than with anything that they could teach them. Not of course that he saw the worst of the pupils for from some obscure sense of fair play they were on their best behaviour when he was sitting there taking notes, knowing that the student was on trial. He shuddered to think what it was like when he wasn't there. How could literature bear the assault of these eyes, these destructive forces?

Mark himself was torn between the calm of the college and the torment of the city. He felt obscurely unclean as if by staying in the college he was sheltering from the "real" world where transactions with evil continued. Like the sophisticates of early centuries who were enmeshed in the idea of the Noble Savage, he felt that his exploration of the world was not deep enough, that his real job ought to be pacification at the very centre. If he had thought that what he was doing was important —or if he had been able to enter into the lives of those who lectured in the college—he wouldn't have felt so disappointed and especially so at the time when he was staying in digs. More and more he was beginning to sense that the day of literature was over, that in a hedonistic time the superficial was king.

What distressed him was the smallness of his colleagues' horizons and the fact that so many of them had surrendered. There was for instance a little man at the head of the Psychology Department who had a small prudent beard and cultivated a vague likeness to D. H. Lawrence. This man offended the students by his megalomaniac attitude and his continual recourse to a book which he had himself written—a yellow book in the series, "Modern Ideas"—and which concerned itself with methods of study and for which a noted psychologist had been induced to write a flattering foreword. There was also an Australian who took the Education Classes and who went in bright and unprepared, simply saying to a class of about eighty girls, "And what do you wish to discuss today?" whereupon there would be a long period of silence gradually punctured by giggles and conversation. And then there was the legendary Speech Specialist who many years before had pointed to the area which produced the glottal stop only to be interrupted by a voice which had shouted gleefully, "And very nice too."

But what Mark missed above all was any sense of dedication to the subject as such. Of course if he could have got into a university this situation would not have arisen. But mainly because of the interruption of National Service he had found himself in that place and had been at first too fascinated to move. But there was no denying the loveliness of the town.

In summer it was quite enchanting with its wide lovely streets, its sparkling air, the fine clean water, the hills seen across the strait. He had in fact fallen in love with it as if it had been a kind of Eden, all the more so as he had just come back from the frustrations and inanities of National Service, with its tedium and ennui, and periods of lying on a barrack bed watching the fall of the rain. True, there had been the terrible Mrs. Walton but in the early days there had also been young lecturers with whom he could discuss literature. But they had all gone, he himself had grown older and was left behind till eventually he had met Lorna.

To marry her was inevitable: there was nothing else he could do. Tired of Mrs. Walton, of digs, he had erupted into a life with Lorna and the more easily because she was alone. If she had brought in her unpredictable wake flotillas of parents, aunts and cousins he would have sheered down the quieter cove to which he had grown used, but in fact, apart from one long haired cousin whom he had never seen, she had brought no retinue with her. The wedding had not been a church one, he had been adamant about that. There had really been a dreadful scene which had ended with her crying helplessly but his honesty had prevailed.

"Why not?" she had shouted. "Why not a church wedding?"

"For the simple reason," he explained patiently, "that I don't go to church. And I don't like to ask favours of anybody."

"What favour? What favour? Other people don't go to church and they have church weddings."

"I'm not other people. I want to be honest about this. If I don't go to church then I won't be dishonest enough to ask for a church wedding. In any case it's all a lot of nonsense. I don't want photographers aiming their cameras at me and people gawking at me in my hired tails which are too long for me."

"I haven't been going to church," said Lorna, "but I want a church wedding. I want to have photographs to look back on. I want to wear a gown."

"You! But you've made fun of the church. I've heard you."

"I know but that's different. I want to be a bride, a real bride." And indeed she did: she wanted to prove that she could be beautiful and radiant like all the other girls she was always talking about—the beautiful models she had met in London, girls with chic, girls who were proud of their bodies, the self worshipping narcissi of the metropolis. Her reading of women's magazines was merely another aspect of what he considered her romanticism.

"No," he repeated obdurately, convinced that he was right. If one wasn't intellectually honest then one wasn't anything. For one terrifying moment he was afraid that she would call off the whole thing (he had visions of returning to the mince and shady rooms of Mrs. Walton), that she would disappear out of his life altogether, that she would simply write to her parents asking for a colossal cheque and take the next train to London. It seemed to him that the parting hung on a hair: but she didn't make the break. Most of the time he couldn't understand what she saw in him anyway. Sometimes she seemed to think that he was an intellectual giant and that nothing was beyond him. Sometimes in the evenings as she sat on the sofa, legs drawn up, watching TV in one of her few moments of perfect stillness he would wonder about it.

She liked running the house. Standing at the cooker, hair all deranged, wearing what looked more like an artist's smock than anything else, she seemed so happy that he often teased her.

"Where do you get this recipe from?"

"I can read, you know. I followed the instructions. That's one thing about your *New Statesman*, there is nothing so common as a recipe there."

"Yes, I've seen you reading them with your tongue hanging out of your mouth."

Actually, when she was drawing, this was what she did, her

tongue did really hang out of her mouth, like a child concentrated on what it is doing. But at the same time he often
felt that she was judging him. After all she had been everywhere, she was a global being, she had met many interesting
people and he envied her that. He envied her that early freedom,
these gipsyish peregrinations. She wouldn't, however, talk
about her early days except when they quarrelled, no matter
how much he probed, and he felt that she was protecting
those years from him in order to nurse them in her memory.
But when they quarrelled she would say things like, "Why have
you taught all these years here then?" And, "You've never
been anywhere. What would you know?" Or she would try
and make him jealous by saying things like, "You should
have seen those officers on the ship."

When they had the painters and decorators in she was in
her element. She could establish a rapport more quickly with
them than he could. She was always running about making
cups of tea for them so that the whole operation became more
expensive than it would otherwise have been. Once she sat on
the stairs with one of them for a whole hour discussing the
diabetes from which the painter suffered and examining the
intricacies of needles and fluid. As for himself he didn't quite
know how to speak to them and wandered from room to room
with his transistor listening to the Test between England and
Australia.

"You know," she said, "the tall one has been all over. He
was an engineer at one time. He was telling me all about
Port Said." He could imagine what he might have been
telling her.

He himself had started the book which Wilkinson had
always been urging on him and was involved in a course of
reading novels in order to prepare himself. It was to be about
Frith whose work he had chosen because he had read a lot
of the novels. Actually most of the novels were about wife
and husband relationships and could be considered in their
entirety as variations on this theme. One, for instance, was
about a writer who had been prevented from attaining his

full power because of the nice wife he had married after a period of spiritual abyss, and had as its epigraph the quotation from Hopkins:

"Let me to my own self be hereafter kind."

Another dealt with the opposite situation; that is, a wife who had been involved in a tempestuous life and had imported into the husband writer's quiet retreat disorderly gales from the world outside.

Sections of the former book were masterly in every way and looked as if they were autobiographical. The prose became luminous with pain as the novelist described the writer's wanderings through midnight streets in a plague of neon.

Mark found that he had really to concentrate on his book for he had fallen into bad habits of superficial reading in the past few years and he had to learn to read again. When he came home from college—which he began to feel as an interruption to his real work—he would start work in his room while Lorna watched TV or occupied herself in some other way that he didn't investigate. In Mark there was a streak of the dissatisfied creative writer. He knew that he could never write a poem or a novel or a play but he felt that he ought to be able to write this particular book, though he was frustrated by not getting in the local public library—run by a dim old man on the point of retirement—the literature that he wanted.

It never entered his head to wonder what Lorna did when he was in college. He simply thought that she would be reading the *Woman's Own* or cooking or watching TV. It was as if she had taken the place of his landlady. But she blossomed too in those early days so that he felt jealous of her. She learned to mow the lawn at the back of the house and she would tell him stories of people she had met when she was out shopping. She had bought herself a bicycle which she would ride on the good summer days instead of taking the car. She would drink coffee in the mornings by herself in a restaurant. But he himself was growing more and more discontented. He felt that something was expected of him that he couldn't provide, that some compensation ought to be made for what she had given up, for instance more companionship. But at the same time he was occupied with his book and felt that what he was doing was useful and likely to have results, though he wasn't very clear what these would be. Now and again she would get letters from her relatives but he would never ask to see them though it turned out that some were from her parents. At one time they were in South Africa rooting for apartheid, at another they were in South America.

"She likes nothing better than night clubs," said Lorna to him once. "Perfectly useless you know" (this she would say with her mouth full of rollers from changing the curtains) "but fabulously beautiful." Unlike this apparently perfect physical being, Lorna had mastered the domestic machinery all right but she was still liable to break things. After getting the hang of a dishwasher or a washing machine she would seem to look to him for approval or praise but he was nearly always preoccupied and never noticed this.

She got on marvellously well with strangers. On summer nights they seemed to come closer together when they would walk along the shore and watch the nostrils of dogs twitching alertly as their owners held the rainbow coloured ball back a second before releasing it. She too wanted a dog but he didn't like dogs and so they didn't get one. On such summer nights she would sit on one of the green benches and immerse herself in conversation with a middle aged women who always haunted the shore and who was telling stories about her son who was a priest "across the water" and her daughter "who was going in for a teacher". Lorna would delight in the quaint talk and imitate the accent, "It's a rer day init?" Sometimes she would take her easel with her and place it on the strip of grass where people usually sat on their wasp striped deckchairs. There she would sit for hours, tongue protruding, her skin turning blacker and blacker in the hot sun, drawing them all, dogs, children, adults running among the blue waves. At times she would be completely dissatisfied and would throw the painting away, watching it drift out to sea. At others she would be quite happy with it. A recurring motif was a black bird that appeared in one corner of the picture. When he asked her about it she told him about the white bird that appears in the later work of Braque. Not that she understood what the bird was there for: her attitude to painting was purely instinctive. Mark's own knowledge of painting was confined to Picasso and Goya and Van Gogh. Once or twice he suggested that they visit the Art Gallery in the city but she wouldn't go. In fact she wouldn't go to the city at all.

But on the whole he was much happier than when he was in digs. He began to grow more and more immersed in his thesis. The prospect of leaving the town took on a sharper reality and he began to withdraw mentally from the college. He saw now quite clearly that the girls were lumpish and uninspired: their work seemed naive, their ambitions petty. Similarly, he found Wilkinson and the rest of the staff mediocre. He began to notice more and more clearly some of the former's habits. Wilkinson would never engage in a conversation about literature with him, and if an argument appeared to be developing he would become aloof in a silly manner. Miss Diamond would talk about Wilkinson behind his back (which Mark would never do) but when he came into the room she was affable again.

Miss Diamond was tall and thin and wore rimless glasses. Her favourite poet was Tennyson. One day Mark was astonished to hear that she still had her university notes and she referred to university professors as if they were gods from Olympus. He once had a discussion with her about "The Lady of Shalott" and found that she hadn't even asked herself the question: What does the poem mean? Why was it written at all? She talked about its "beauty" and shortly afterwards launched into a tirade against the Geography man who was trying to import into the library a massive American book which would cost ten guineas.

"How he expects me to know about these books I don't understand. I think he's mad actually. Have you noticed his moustache? I should expect him to marry at any moment.

Have you noticed how he's been trimming his moustache recently? And his teeth. Whiter than white. You should hear him boasting to the girls about his career. And he's only got a second class too. Did you know that he shifted his university half way through but it didn't do him any good?"

It seemed that in this atmosphere literature itself was going sour on Mark. It was as if for the first time he realised how few people were interested in it: how the world was run by grey men who emerged like crocodiles from a swamp. He felt that in some way he had been conned, that the serious had turned into the frivolous, that what was deadly earnest had turned into play, that poetry itself was going the way of theology, either into meaningless linguistics or into the glare of pop. Now and again he felt a deadly constriction as if all that he believed in was in deadly danger, as if he had mistaken the froth on the surface for the lethal churnings below.

One day Wilkinson summoned them in and said gravely like Eisenhower at D Day: "They are going to build an extension to the college. At the present moment it looks as if the Science and Music Departments will benefit most but I feel strongly that we should have a room suitable for theatrical purposes and the showing of films. I have drawn up a document which I should like you to read."

He passed an impeccably typed document round the table (all his "plans" were impeccably typed and the language florid and impersonal). They all looked at it, Mark and Miss Diamond and Mr. Gray who was a large friendly stertorous man who spilt ash on his waistcoat most of the time and was an ex-Cambridge graduate. The document was impressively phrased with sentences beginning with "It is felt . . ." and "It is considered" and so on which detached it from the sordid greed of the personal and placed it in the Platonic realms of the ideal. Somewhere up there there was an umpire who "it was believed" wished that Wilkinson should get his room.

Mark could see no relationship between the contents of the document and the reality of the department. He knew for a fact that Wilkinson was entirely uninterested in both the theatre and the cinema and never visited either. His favourite film was *Rebecca* which he had seen many years before. It was with a remoteness that bordered on indifference that Mark read the paper, arranged and numbered point after point like a military document of the kind that Wilkinson might have seen when he was serving in Africa during the war. How could Wilkinson actually and in cold blood write this? How could he not see the gap between reality and appearance? It was purely a ploy in power politics. It was a document which he could admire and keep, the only outlet for his minimal creativity, an aesthetic object like the examination papers he set and spent such time over. Like a child he wanted to have a part of what was going. It was quite likely (indeed more than likely) that even if he got the room he wouldn't use it as a theatre. It would however be part of the Department. It would be another area that Wilkinson would be able to call his own.

For a moment Mark studied him, the craggy face, the tall rangy body. The eyes were wrinkled as if he were one of those Americans who look across immense distances towards a dim frontier. He radiated benevolent energy and believed implicitly in the value of what he was doing. In fact, thought Mark, he should have been a farmer. He was in the habit of giving long notes to his classes and would tell them little anecdotes such as one may hear in a theatre from a poor comedian trying to warm up his audience. For instance, if he was discussing Sophocles he would tell them how he had been to Greece in the war and what the Greeks were like and what they ate and what they drank and seemed to be convinced that this would cast a perfect illumination over a tragedy that had occurred even before men were born.

Mark felt cowardly in not stating his thoughts about the room. Miss Diamond of course was all for extending the domain. Mr. Gray made no objection but, as his asthma concealed effectively whether his vague heavings constituted yes or no, no-one ever really listened to him and he didn't expect that anyone would. Mark said nothing and merely watched Wilkinson who ticked off point after point with a gold pencil.

Mark had a vague vision of each of them running to their planes after the briefing was over, and taking off into the blue skies of the Battle of Britain. He found Wilkinson incomprehensible. Yet Wilkinson would be considered by most people as a competent man. Mark remembered a Company Sergeant Major he had once encountered in the army. This man was extremely idle but at all parades and sports meetings he would be met striding across square and field carrying an impressive file of notes and documents tied with an elastic band and he would look extremely hard pressed and busy, encased in a local air of urgency. For this reason even if one knew that he was bone lazy one might wonder whether this time perhaps he was doing something of value.

This was exactly how he felt about Wilkinson. Now Miss Diamond was talking about shifting the library to the new block which would be rather distant from the Geography Department. The new building had become a focus for their various futures. Mark amused himself by sketching in a new Lady of Shalott where Wilkinson would, all a-glitter, cross the field of corn and Miss Diamond, ravished away from her mirror, would lie down in a boat and float down to the college which was her Camelot, and Wilkinson would stand on the bank looking down at her distraught face saying, "Yes, she did try." So they talked on about the new building till eventually everyone forgot what it was intended for. It was a speculative place, a new beginning, it was itself and not its use, it was the façade that rose in their imagination concealing reality.

(3)

Lorna started going to church mainly because of Mrs. Carmichael who stayed next door with her husband who was a doctor with a large body and a burnt face. He played rugby for a local team. Of course there might have been other reasons for her wishing to go to church, but if so she didn't tell Mark. Mark himself had no intention of ever going to church, and felt that Lorna had in some way betrayed both him and herself. He felt rather bewildered when he saw her putting on her green coat and her green hat and beginning to appear less untidy than she had been.

Mrs. Carmichael was older than Lorna – about thirty-five – but she was neat and trim and interested in doing good works. She would often make tablet for sales of work and grew flowers in her garden for the church. But she wasn't at all a stupid woman and not at all the kind who runs after the minister. Indeed she was neither servile nor stuffy. When they came first she would leave things at the door for them in a basket, mainly fruit and jam which she had made herself. She was more educated than the usual good woman for once or twice after she started visiting them Mark had an argument with her and she was quite capable of holding her own, though she did tend to stammer a little when she got excited

Mark himself knew a little about theology for he read indiscriminately. He sensed that the theologians were beginning to surrender and wanted to be liked, for, after all, there they were, complete from university or college, and there was nothing for them to do, for no-one wanted to hear what they had to say. Therefore, like artists, they must be lonely people. Their abandonment of God he thought of as ridiculous, but perhaps it was no more so than the abandonment of strict form by the poets. They retreated into a language which bristled with abstract words, so that one picked one's way through it with the greatest difficulty.

But, as for Mrs. Carmichael, Lorna seemed to look on her as an older sister. They would go for early morning coffee together and little by little Lorna grew more dependent on her for companionship. Mark didn't like her much: to him she represented the bourgeois, the more so as she was more modern than was consistent with the ethics of the bourgeoisie. And yet there was no reason why he should dislike her. After all what was wrong with doing "good works"? There must be people in the world who needed help. But in the same way as he was suspicious of people who went on long walks to help save Vietnam from napalm, he was suspicious of her because she was doing something that he would never think of doing himself.

Mrs. Carmichael wasn't exactly a blue stocking. She was a highly personable, indeed attractive, woman who had decided that service for others was of the greatest importance. It amazed Mark that Lorna had taken up with her, for her environment and breeding were all against such an association. Lorna was arty and scatterbrained while Mrs. Carmichael was a very organised woman. Lorna had actually never been to church in her life before and surprisingly became attached to going. She talked about the silence of the church, about the coolness, about the kindness of the people, how they shook her hand when the service was over, how there was no pressure on her to go. She even liked the church artistically with its blue cloth draped over the pulpit and the great red cross at the front.

Lorna and Mrs. Carmichael had got hold of a hermit whom they were helping. This had happened after they had started going to a small discussion group with the minister, a pleasant man who had preached in Africa before coming home. When they went to the hermit's house first he was living in incredible filth, according to Lorna, but they had cleaned the place out (the doctor giving them a great deal of advice) and he was now more comfortable, though liable to snarl at them when he was in a bad temper. Once he had threatened to throw them out of the house, but Mrs. Carmichael's invincible good temper had prevailed. Lorna didn't care for his ingratitude and was for giving up but Mrs. Carmichael had explained the psychology of the hermit to her. He hated them because they were doing good and that was a great weight on his mind. One night Mark and Mrs. Carmichael had a great argument about the hermit. Mark said: "One day I was on a bus tour and the driver stopped at a small tin hut at the side of the road. It had a rather clumsy chimney, I remember. The driver blew his horn and after a while this hermit came out. His braces were tied round his trousers like a belt and he looked as if he had just got out of bed though it was twelve o'clock. He was carrying a chanter in his hand and he came and stood on the steps of the bus. He had a rather professional line in patter and he told the passengers how every Tuesday he went down the road for his pension. He said he used to poach in the past but he had stopped that now as he was getting too old. He also told us how the TV people had been trying to interview him. He played some tunes on his chanter, very badly, I may say. The women were all agog about him, inventing all sorts of romantic backgrounds for him. One big fat Yorkshire woman kept insisting that it was "luv" that had driven him into a hermit's life.

"When the driver sent round the hermit's tin at the end for money I couldn't see any reason why I should give him any. After all he did play the chanter very badly and really he was also a colossal bore. In any case, if he was a hermit why was he making money from innocent passengers? He seems to me to have been merely an inadequate man."

"And so you think," said Mrs. Carmichael, "that I'm wasting my time with the hermit?"

"If he's a real hermit he shouldn't want you and in any case how do you know you're making him any happier?"

"Well, at least he's cleaner than he was, as far as I can gather," said her husband calmly smoking his pipe. "And that's always something. Cleanliness, you know, does make a difference to people."

"He was dying," said Lorna. "He would have died if we hadn't helped him. All you do is go around with your *New Statesman* mentality which means that you end up doing nothing at all except criticise."

But Mark continued, "Who gave you the right to go and help him? That's what I don't understand. The question is asked in all seriousness."

"And all humility don't forget," said Lorna bitterly. "All you want is an argument. You're just listening to yourself talking."

"Oh I can quite see what your husband is getting at," said Mrs. Carmichael. Lorna got up furiously and went into the kitchen to make some tea.

"Well I don't," she said on her way out, "I can't see it at all. He's just making mischief. The fact is he doesn't want to soil his lily white hands."

"Do you mean," said the doctor, "that we have no right to help each other?" Surely that is putting it a bit strong. After all what would my job be like if that was the case? I wouldn't have a job at all," he said looking round him with a comic air.

"That's different," said Mark, "they come to ask for your help. I'm talking about people like my wife imposing herself on others."

"And me," said Mrs. Carmichael.

"All right then. What's your answer?" And he smiled at her in order to take the sting out of the words.

"Mark, have you ever been lonely?" said Mrs. Carmichael. "I mean, really lonely."

"Of course he hasn't been," said Lorna from the kitchen. "He's never been alone in London as I have and, believe me, that's loneliness. He hasn't lived at all."

Mark considered and said at last, "Yes, I have been lonely."

"Absolutely alone?" said Mrs. Carmichael. "I don't mean intellectually alone but really alone so that you don't have anyone at all to talk to."

"No, I can't say that I have been that. But then your hermit chose to be alone. You at his moment of weakness have chosen to break into his loneliness. What will happen when you leave him? Won't he be worse off than ever?"

"That, I suppose, is a valid point," said the doctor looking at his wife.

"Oh, it's a valid point right enough," said Mrs. Carmichael. "But then the world is full of valid points." Before she could continue, Lorna came in with tea and biscuits and said,

"A valid point. That's the jargon of the *New Statesman*. What's valid about it? He's talking about valid points as if this was an argument which didn't relate to anything. The man was filthy. He was in bed: he couldn't move. There was no-one to feed him but us. He's unshaven and dirty. He's never seen TV in his life. He hasn't got a radio. He lives all by himself. Utterly. It's high time you got into the real world, Mark."

"But what is the 'real world'? The world of the hermit? Surely you aren't going to say that that is the real world? That's what you seem to be defending."

Lorna distributed tea and biscuits and said, "Anyway I'm not going to argue with you. I get satisfaction from what I'm doing though at the beginning I hated his guts. He's more comfortable than he has been for years. Mark," she said to the other two, "doesn't understand why I'm doing this. He doesn't seem to realise the uselessness of my life. I never did anything for anybody before, not in my whole life. When I wanted to go somewhere I went and asked my father for my cheque and that was that. If I wanted a new hat or a new coat I did the same. I was completely futile."

"And I always thought you an iconoclastic artist," said Mark. "You married me under false pretences."

"Don't we all do that?" said Mrs. Carmichael. "Surely you aren't blaming her for turning out to be better than you expected."

"I don't know," said Mark, "I feel that this hermit is very important. He's a symbol of some kind. There he is, escaped as he thinks from the world, but other people impose on him whether he wants to or not at the moment when he is incapable of resisting them. Is the world jealous that he has succeeded so long in doing without it?"

"Perhaps he's had enough of his loneliness after all," said Lorna. "Perhaps he really wants to be helped."

"You'd be surprised how many of his type there are even in a beautiful town like this," said Mrs. Carmichael. "You'd be surprised how many people suffer great griefs and need help. Most of them are grateful, some are not. I'm not setting myself up as a Florence Nightingale. But we do live in a community after all."

"I agree," said the doctor. "I was talking to a hotel keeper the other night. He had just had this hotel built and he was telling me about how he had it furnished and decorated. He told me that the local firm charged higher prices than a city firm would but he felt it was his duty to support his community, so he hired them anyway. I thought that rather admirable. It shows you that in a small town cut-throat business ethics don't apply."

"It doesn't, of course, show anything of the sort," said his wife gently. "It only shows that he sees a good bit further than some hotel keepers would do. He makes sure that you know about it, you'll tell someone else, and so he'll be patronised."

"That's true," said the doctor, taking the pipe out of his mouth. "I must say I hadn't thought of that. Mind you, I admit that this town like any other small town is a hive of gossip. People, I believe, are good on the whole, but, on the other hand, they can be nasty too. Still, surely it is a good thing that you should help the hermit. After all, it takes energy and there are other things you might have been doing. You could be going to the cinema for instance or playing bingo."

"And spending Mark's hard earned money," said Lorna. So the discussion continued aimlessly as such discussions do, eventually coming to the confrontation which is: Who is the more admirable man, the one who, corrupted, fights in the arena or the one who, uncorrupted, looks on?

When the Carmichaels had gone, Lorna said to him, "I don't know why you always have to argue with people. Why can't you just talk? You never seem to be able to talk about anything without turning it into an argument."

"Well, I used to tell you all about my girl students but you didn't want to hear."

"What bosh," said Lorna. "I wouldn't hear anything at all if I relied on you. After all, people are interesting."

"Are they?"

"Yes they are, though you seem to have become an aristocrat."

"I thought you were the aristocrat."

"I don't know about that but I like people better than you do. Did you know for instance that the local headmaster has had to leave because he was beating his wife? You didn't know that, did you?"

"No, and what has that knowledge contributed to my understanding of the world?"

Later when they got into bed, he said, "I'm sorry. It's just that Mrs. Carmichael makes me argue. She doesn't mind."

"How do you know she doesn't?"

"Well she is really rather an intelligent person after all."

"Intelligence? That's what you always think about, isn't it? If people aren't intelligent then they are no use to you."

"I wouldn't say that. There are many ways of being intelligent. But I must say that I prefer it to your so-called niceness."

"Well, I don't know why you married me. I'm not intelligent."

"Let's not be proud of it then."

Later still he said, "Look, I'll apologise to Mrs. Carmichael if you like. It's just that I don't seem to be making much headway with my book and that makes me irritable."

He paused and then said, "By the way, do you remember that night I was at your flat, you had a pile of Sunday *Observers* and *Timeses*. And a novel by Henry James. Did you read them?"

"Of course not. I bought them just to impress you. I thought that you might like Henry James. All the intelligentsia are always talking about him at parties."

He was amazed that she should have done this.

"But why should you have bothered to do that?" he asked.

"Because I liked you. One must be insincere sometimes, if one likes someone."

The window of the bedroom was open and he could smell the perfume from the garden. Undressing, she appeared like a ghostly flower in the darkness, luminous and mushroomy.

"You're changing," he said. "You're growing up." He felt a terrible envy as if he himself were incapable of change and that some cataclysm would have to strike before he could move in any direction. She reminded him of a poem he had read by someone about Persephone emerging in the spring from the earth, diaphanous and ghostly, a root breaking, an unpredictable blossom, a purple crown.

The green watch on his naked arm was like a picture of earth and he gazed at it—time passing—with a distant love and fear. She was so young and he was old. She was capable of becoming someone else. He felt for the first time a strangeness deep in his heart, a foreshadowing of autumnal ice such as one sometimes senses in the air at the close of summer, a constriction of the heart when one stands in front of the mirror in the bathroom with the used blade and the lukewarm water.

(4)

The city—about seven miles from the town in which Mark stayed—was changing all the time in the Wilson era. Where once there had been slums there were now housing estates: there was more space opening out as mouldy rotten warm houses were dragged to the earth. Great slabs of multi-storey flats rose against the low red industrial sky. Sometimes he imagined what it must have been like in the past, the warm closeness of people, the flare of the blue gas at the stairhead, the trams, the men shouting from their piles of oranges and apples in the open air, the music hall, the earthy jokes, the flat caps.

Now it was changing. It was becoming lighter, airier, colder. There was more glass in the shops. Roads were widening, bridges soared above the city. There was a sparkle where there once had been a density. He had images in his mind of people walking close together in the past, of doors opening and shutting to let neighbours in, of huge red women standing underneath clothes lines, pegs in their mouths, their large red arms stretching upwards towards the billowing blue and white. He had a certain nostalgia for this time though he had never experienced it. It seemed to be full of Irish people, and policemen with moustaches running after the intrepid Celts like long lines of glue on a bad TV screen. It was also a time of surprises, when trains turned into hosepipes, and doors into stars rotating.

Now it was changing. Density was being replaced by an open precariousness symbolised by the Belisha Beacons, by the winking of lights. Lounges replaced open pubs, leather seats of black and red replaced wooden ones, ashtrays replaced spitoons. And the face behind the knife was cold, not warm. It was expressionless without passion. It was a diagram, not a living being.

One day, after he had endured a lesson with a particularly dim girl, Mark went into the main railway station bar in the city for a drink. It was students' charity day and he had been accosted by a number of students who were carrying a coffin with a girl in it, while written on the outside were the words, "Pay to open this box." It was a cold day but the students reminded him of his own university days many years before when he had gone about the streets clinking his can and asking people for money and making the kind of joke that students do make on such occasions. It was on charities day—a particularly hot May day—that, weary and satisfied with his work in a good cause, he had gone into a bar for the first drink of beer that he had ever taken.

Now, the students came into the railway bar and the customers in good humour—for there was a Celtic–Rangers match that day—bantered with them and contributed generously. As he stood at the bar drinking his rum—a blue scarf practically trailing into his glass—he saw not far from him a person he recognised: it was in fact a writer he had once met at a symposium which he had attended and this writer had been giving a talk on the novel. He was a smallish abrasive man with a black moustache whom he remembered as a rather iconoclastic speaker. He had made a good impression with his nervous urgency and bluntness. For instance he had maintained that he wrote his novels not for the critics but for ordinary people: he said that he had no time for experimentalism and that the great Russian novelists—who were of course the supreme exponents of the art—were not experimentalists either but wrote about human beings in situations of crisis. He wanted in effect a spiritual content in his work. In the discussion afterwards a number of people had taken him up on this point of experimentalism, asking him what he thought of James Joyce, whom he did not agree was a great novelist, much to their surprise.

So when Mark saw him standing by himself with a glass of beer in his hand he went over to him. At first he didn't recognise Mark but when the latter remanded him of the talk (to which Mark himself had contributed some passionate remarks) he greeted him warmly enough. He seemed to Mark to look even more peaked than when he had seen him before. It turned out however that he had been entirely consistent in his ideas of realism, for in the previous year or two he had been involved in a project for the dispossessed and the delinquent in the worst areas of the city. He was doing this not so much to get material for a new novel but to prevent himself from retiring into an ivory tower where he would become obsessed not by human problems but by language. He spoke as fiercely and nervously as ever:

"The trouble is that most novelists go and look for so-called experiences which they then turn into novels. Their books are just travelogues." (Here he named one or two of those novelists.) They were interrupted at this point by a young man who was looking for a ticket for the big match and who was willing to give five pounds for it. Mark told him he didn't have a ticket but the young man was rather obstreperous till Hunter (for that was the name of the novelist) gave him a long look and he disappeared muttering something about these bloody Prods."

"As I was saying," said Hunter calmly, "these books are just travelogues. I don't know whether I'll ever write a book about this project but that's certainly not why I agreed to take part in it."

"What is it like?" said Mark, buying him a whisky and thinking at the same time that Hunter didn't look the sort of person who would be taking part in a project which involved such tough delinquents.

"What's it like?" Hunter repeated, smiling and looking at Mark as if he was one of those people who wanted to write what he called travelogues, a tourist of the human distress. "It's difficult to say. They have their own rules, you know. That's the first thing to understand. It's not an anarchic society. It's like learning to grow antennae. If you make a mistake, if you say the wrong thing, do the wrong thing . . ." He made a gesture of cutting his throat. "You can't imagine how hard you have to concentrate. In fact it's like trying to learn a language while going through a minefield at the same time. The thing is of course that you and I and anyone else who had to live where they live would grow up exactly like them. That's what the so-called TV commentators forget. We've had a belly-ful of them, always poking their noses and cameras in looking for stories. It's all survival technique."

He paused for a moment. "It's hard to explain. It's like being on another world. All those waste lands, those huge estates, like being on the moon. They're moon men."

Mark thought grimly about Mrs. Carmichael and wondered what she would do, if she would march in there, the banners of principle and Barth held high.

"They're doomed of course," said Hunter. "That's the ter-rible thing, they're doomed. Which means that literally they have no future. None at all. There's little you can do. You can't save them. They've gone beyond anything anyone can do for them. They're completely unpredictable, you see. They'll attack you for no reason at all. Suddenly one of them will go for a hatchet and then go for you and then it's you or him. There's a hostility there all the time beneath the surface and they're looking at you all the time, studying you. They don't understand you of course but they *try* to understand you by external signs, the way you walk, the clothes you wear. When they attack you they're not attacking you really. For that moment you happen to be in their way, that's all. They live in the present, totally." He brooded for a moment into his whisky. "They show no affection whatsoever you see. That's the terrifying thing." He stared past Mark as if on to the waste planet of which he had been talking. "No affection at all. They think of no-one but themselves, or rather they don't think of themselves. What their minds must be like is inconceivable to our so-called liberals. They hate any show of affection and of course you must never help for "social" reasons. They're very suspicious of that. They're so prickly and sensitive it's not true. They hate to touch each other or be touched. The only thing they'll touch you with is a weapon." He looked into Mark's face as if he were trying to work something out, as if he saw even there that remoteness and coldness. "I'll tell you, I've got a theory about them. I believe that knives are their form of communication. Do you believe that? Knives are for them a form of love."

"Love?"

"Yes, they communicate with knives as normal people with their hands and lips. They are hollow inside, you see. Debris. The landscape around them has penetrated them. Their minds are as empty as slums and the lighting is bloody awful. Primitive. And yet as I say they have rules. You could probably walk in there and they wouldn't attack you because they don't recognise you as belonging to a gang. But if you did belong to a gang and they suspected it, God help you."

"Did you earn their respect?" said Mark, sipping his third rum and trying to get away from a large man who was elbowing his way towards the bar.

"Respect? What does that mean? You might earn their tolerance for a while. But respect. They respect nothing. Everything that they have ever tried to hang on to has been taken away from them. It's very exhausting being with them for you have to start from the beginning every time. To communicate with them at all is an achievement. That's why I found that literary talk I gave so unreal. Playing with words." He was silent for a moment and then he continued again. Mark looked down at his rum as if it were blood.

"The fact is I can't write about them even if I wanted to. How could anyone write about them? All the normal procedures disintegrate when you're confronted by that. Fiction assumes that the world is reasonable. These people aren't. You would have to postulate a world on the analogy of magic;

that is, anything can happen at any time. They don't have continuous characters, you see."

"And they show no affection at all?" said Mark. "That's odd. I thought that they were very physical. I mean when I was in the army, all these people used to talk about women all the time. It was really quite obscene as you know. Their talk was absolutely and without qualification about women. I can never remember them talking about anything else."

"Not this lot. I'm telling you they're like robots. They're killers. Sometimes you can't even see any expression at all on their faces. No-one can save them. They don't trust anybody. Nothing can get through to them. It's like walking through No Man's Land."

His eyes gazed into the distance and Mark felt frightened and excited at the same time. He imagined a No Man's Land with these people moving about in it like wolves, green-eyed, hating, competent with knives and claws. What would Mrs. Carmichael make of them, bringing her gifts? It was all right to go and clean out a hermit's house but out there was the real lightning . . .

"Look, let's get out of here, it's too crowded," said Hunter.

They left the pub and started walking. All around them the city was being dismantled. Huge office blocks towered above them: in the rigging of buildings workmen clung like sailors singing their pop songs. Mark imagined the ancient closes with their blue gas lighting, the women in their long skirts. Now however there were the miniskirted beauties of the sixties, with their thighs freezing. Cinemas showed not Charlie Chaplin but sexy Scandinavian films where young boys and girls camped by acreages of water and stripped moonily outside ghostly tents. No story, just mood.

"You were saying about rules," Mark said. They passed a tall thin man wearing kid gloves and Hunter looked after him briefly as if he were some strange antique being emerged out of history.

"Yes," he answered, "there is only one reason why they won't attack a person who has been in an opposing gang. Do you know what that reason is?"

"No," said Mark.

"Well, they won't attack him if he's married. To them he has become a drop out once he marries."

"How do people become like that?" said Mark. "I mean without affection."

"Become like that? I don't know. Nobody knows. Housing schemes. Broken families. You know it's a funny thing, when I go to these stupid 'Matters of Opinion' that people have they always ask you, 'Do you believe in the death penalty?' The thing is that the death penalty is only used against people who harm others physically but think of all those people who harm others mentally, and twist their minds and make them grow up warped. Surely the death penalty should be applied to them as well."

"The point is," Hunter continued, switching to a theme which obviously interested him, "how to find words for people who have no words, for whom language doesn't even begin to exist, people who don't have any emotions at all."

Yes, thought Mark, Wilkinson was like that. He had no sensitivity, no real emotions. Long ago anything that was intellectual and fine in him had disintegrated in the struggle for petty power. Must the world always be like that? He watched a frail old woman quivering like a compass needle at a zebra crossing in a series of small panics.

Mark felt intense admiration for this young writer who had gone into the inferno with no weapons but his concern and courage. Three youths in leather jackets swaggered towards them, their green scarves cleaner than the rest of their clothes. They were singing. All the pedestrians carefully turned their faces away from them and looked blankly into the grey day.

"What did you actually do?" he asked.

"Oh, we organised dances and we stopped fights. They can't argue rationally of course. An argument is an extension of the personality. If you lose an argument then that is a diminution of your personality. At least that is the way their minds work."

Part of Mark yearned at that moment to be with Lorna, part longed to be in the blue light where these figures moved in what was the ultimate truth, that which went beyond argument, beyond discussion, beyond literature.

"I don't suppose I could go along with you some time," he said.

"You mean as a tourist?" said Hunter ironically.

"No not really. Just to understand, that's all." To be quenched, that was it.

"So you suffer from the ennui of words then," said Hunter smiling bitterly. "You teach in some college or other, don't you?"

"Yes."

"Well, all right then. We'll fix a date. Drop me a note. Here's the address."

That over, Mark said, "What do you think about Frith's work? Do you read him much? I'm working on a thesis about him."

"Frith? He was pretty good ages ago, I believe, but I never read him now. He was a bit of an ivory tower man, wasn't he?"

"Ivory tower? Surely not. What about that first book and the one called *Night without Stars*? I'm beginning to think that he's the greatest writer we've produced."

"So they say," said Hunter, carelessly letting his eyes follow the smart tight bottom of a miniskirted girl.

"But don't you think so?"

"To be frank with you I haven't read enough of his work to pass a judgment. Did he become a Christian or something?"

"Christian? Of course not. Listen, I know of no-one who writes as he does. Some of his paragraphs move me to tears. He's got a section in particular where the husband is just leaving after he and his wife have agreed to a divorce. It's marvellous. I only wish I could remember the words. But it turns on his touching his hall table just as he's leaving. And he's suddenly thinking that he's leaving his prints there as he's done so often before. I thought it was terrific. You talk about tenderness. Well, he' s certainly got that. What about that story about the artist? 'He touched the flesh which became marble in his hands.' There's something like that in Seferis," said

Mark, watching a red bus lurching past, the stone lions mouthing soundlessly from the square, the twin yellow swords poised above.

"Sorry," said Hunter, 'I prefer football myself. I don't mean that in any derogatory sense. I think it's healthier, that's all. Did you see those characters with the leather jackets? They'll go to Ibrox and they'll yell their heads off. What art could create that feeling in them? And what art is more beautiful, more passionate, more unpredictable, than football? There are whole novels contained in one game of football, heroism, cowardice, the lot. That's the only thing the delinquents I was talking about are interested in. That's the only thing that'll wake them up. Come on, let's go and get something to eat. I'll tell you something. The highest form of excellence we've created in the last decade is Celtic Football Club. And I mean it."

(5)

Continually his dissatisfaction with the college grew. All the freshness had gone from his lectures and he found himself losing his sense of humour. He was making irritating errors of a minor nature. Notices came round which he never read or which he ticked off with self-destructive casualness. Often he found himself standing at the window looking out, saying nothing at all. For after all what was there to say? What terrified him more than anything was that he was beginning to lose faith in literature itself. He knew that if that happened there would be nothing at all left. Words began to lose their power, texts to merge into each other. He contrasted the schoolgirls in front of him with the delinquents of whom he had been told by Hunter. They lived as he did in a favoured climate. What right had he to be teaching at all, unless words could be used as weapons? How would they help him at the very ultimate? If someone close to one died—the breathing becoming short and quick, the eyes becoming panic-stricken—

would he be able to sit beside him into the watches of the night holding up a copy of Dante in order to give meaning to that death?

Notes would come round from Wilkinson which he never read. He felt as if he himself was already a posthumous being, luminous with decay. Sometimes he thought of Lorna with her hermit and of Mrs. Carmichael with her simple belief in a goodness which had never really been tested. Would Barth himself, encased in his armour of theology, walk through those midnight streets where the lights were blue and the knives flashed and figures without affection swarmed in their terrible packs?

Once after he had been to see Wilkinson about books the latter called him back and said, fiddling with a large green paperweight on his desk:

"Is there anything wrong?"

"Wrong? What should be wrong?"

"You don't seem to be so happy these days. You used to brim over with ideas."

"Nothing. There's nothing wrong."

"I'm not complaining you understand but I feel there is something wrong. You're all right at home are you?"

"Of course," he said coldly. "Interfering bugger," he muttered under his breath.

"The thing is I'd come to depend on you. You were always so full of ideas. As you know, I'm not an ideas man myself. I'm just an administrator and I know you despise administrators." The dim shrewd eyes gazed into his own.

"I'm writing a book," he said at last. "I'm taking your advice. And I'm keeping rather late nights over it."

"You're writing a book, eh? That's good, that's good. What's it called? I'm very pleased to hear that."

"I haven't given it a title yet. It's a thesis."

"Oh I'm very glad to hear that, very glad indeed. But don't waste the midnight oil. We are only human, you know, and there is so much to do here, so much. Sometimes, indeed often, I feel that we're not doing enough. One feels a terrible responsibility, whether one is doing the right thing, and whether one is doing enough."

"I'm having difficulty with the book, that's all."

"Well if that's all." Wilkinson looked at him doubtfully and then continued. "What do you think of my latest suggestions for putting forward our plans?"

"They seem reasonable enough," said Mark.

"You agree then that we should get some backing from the parents?" said Wilkinson looking at him sharply.

"Why not? It's as good a way as any."

"That's precisely why I'm worried about you," said Wilkinson getting to his feet and approaching him. I didn't suggest that at all. I would never dream of approaching them. You haven't read my notes at all, have you?"

"I haven't been feeling too well."

"In that case . . ." Wilkinson looked at him thoughtfully as he muttered something and left. There was something odd going on, Wilkinson thought, though he couldn't think what it was: perhaps Mark should never have got married in the first place. However, surely at his age he must know what he was doing. That wife of his of course was a bit young and a bit arty. Then he began to think about the Head of the Science Department who was definitely going to kick up a fuss about the allocation of space in the new building. He wondered if perhaps it would be possible to outmanoeuvre him by an alliance with the Music man, who was nice and idealistic and unpractical, whereas the Science man was very dynamic and abrasive and new to the job. And of course Science nowadays was far more prestigious than the Arts. Naturally if he went to Holmes he would just say with that beatific expression of his, "My hands are tied," and you always went away feeling sorry for him.

Wilkinson felt a bit inferior to Mark who seemed to read far more than he did. All he had time for was the *Times Literary Supplement* whose reviews he read with great care. Mark seemed actually to read the books but then he didn't have to do any administration. He felt sorry for Mark and genuinely concerned for him. He decided that he must ask him and his wife to dinner soon.

Meanwhile Mark was back at his class, thinking about 'that cut price Machiavellian, Wilkinson'. He wasn't above setting traps, was he? He stared dully at the girls, fixed in his swamp of apathy and feeling that he had got the infection from them. What use would they ever make of what he told them? The day of the specialist was over, or at least that's what it said in the *Encounter* article he had read recently. Homer lay forever dead in his grave and all the Graeco-Roman civilisation with him. The Roman and Greek skies were turning cloudy and invaded by random blanknesses. It was the hour of the mediocre and the superficial striking all over the world. The intricate, the enigmatic and the civilised were finished.

When his particular hour was over he went to the nearest pub and asked for a whisky, sitting there on a black leather covered seat watching some local youths playing darts and eating large proletarian pies in the interval. He couldn't understand what was happening to him. It was as if he were surrounded by a continual fog. There was no-one he could talk to and he realised that by withdrawing from the neighbouring society such as it was, he was becoming very lonely indeed, a loneliness which his marriage hadn't cured. If he were only a revolutionary . . . But in the sunny day with the deckchairs strewn along the front such a thought was merely ludicrous. All that had happened was that his marriage had brought him new responsibilities. Lorna was not the kind of person he had taken her for. There she was going about with Mrs. Carmichael, stabilising herself, fitting herself into this world. She had insisted on becoming a woman.

A squat man with a glass of stout came and sat down beside him. "A foine day, sor," he said and Mark agreed. The Irishman was one of those wanderers who worked on the local hydro-electric scheme earning fifty pounds a week and about another fifty in danger money. He lived with his workmates in dormitories and most of the money he earned was spent on mindless marathon gambling sessions.

"Is there much violence?" Mark wondered on his second whisky.

"Violence sor? There's fighting sor, if that's what you're meaning. A fellow was killed there the other day."

"Oh, how did that happen?"

"Well, sor, it was like this. This fellow—Murphy his name was and he came from Donegal—was saying that a hurley pitch was longer than a football pitch. And the other fellow—Patton his name is—argued with him. Well, so the argument went on and on and then Patton took out a knife and did him."

"I see. Just for that."

"Yes, sor. Course people will argue about anything."

"Do you get a lot of killing then?" said Mark.

"Not killing, sor, so much as fighting. It's surprising the amount of that you get. Mind you, most of the fellows are friendly enough except when they get a bit of drink in them."

"Do you get home to Ireland yourself much?"

"Sometimes sor I go over at Christmas but most of the fellows aren't married, see. They go about from place to place. So they've got nothing to go home for. I'm a married man meself and I would like a job back in the ould country but there's no help for it. We get people from all over at the camp. There's a fellow from Yugoslavia. He can't go back home for the Commies."

"Do you like the work then?"

"You've got to, sor, haven't you? There's nothing else for it. You've got to put up with it. Mind you, I would like a job inside, meself. I'm getting on now. But I wasn't clever enough."

A youth came and put a coin in the purple juke box which stood at the far end of the room. The song blasted through the pub, sobbing, wailing, the contortions of what seemed a genuine passion. Mark liked Bob Dylan and the ballads but he couldn't make up his mind about pop though he had seen on the sleeves of records words of songs which appeared authentically poetic. Similarly he liked Westerns on TV or in the cinema but would never read one.

The Irishman left him to go and talk to some of his friends who had just come in. Mark bought another whisky and sat in the corner looking round him. He didn't want to go back and continue work on his book as he felt that he wasn't getting anywhere with it. He just wanted to sit there and drink, something he had not done during broad daylight before. There were a number of visitors in the room and finally he found himself talking to an insurance inspector who had come to the town on business and who surprisingly enough was interested in literature. He sat there till tea time drinking whisky after whisky and arrived home rather fuzzy. Lorna didn't say anything but looked at him with a rather grim expression on her face. He spent the next hours typing and throwing away what he had typed. Nothing that he wrote seemed at all real. Nothing that he thought seemed real either. When Lorna came in to tell him about the tea she found him lying on the bed half asleep, his jacket off but his shoes still on.

(6)

One day, in pursuit of Lorna's painting, she drove him and herself down to a small village which was about twenty miles from the town where they stayed. When they arrived they parked the car beside the only hotel which stood by the through road and walked down to the shore past a small shop where Mark bought a copy of Le Carre's *The Spy who Came in from the Cold*. Mark had of course been there before and pointed out to her the roses climbing up the sides of the houses. The village was one of the most beautiful in Scotland and represented to him all that was protected and old world and nice. It made one think of long afternoons in the sun and honey for tea with its weight of flowers set against a background of trees.

It looked almost like an English village though there were no thatched houses.

They sat down at the water, watching the small boats careering over the loch in which the shadows of the mountains massed at the edges, while in the centre there was a white glitter. On the far side Mark could see deer walking. Half naked boys walked about, slapping their wet feet on the brittle wood of the pier. There were a number of city boys in tight trousers hanging about.

Lorna set up her easel and began to paint. Mark wandered off to find the little church which wasn't far from the shore. He didn't go inside but studied the names on the gravestones in the churchyard, many of which went back centuries. The hot sun beat down on his head and neck, and bees hummed around. A little girl and boy played hide and seek among the graves. Beside the church-yard a stream flowed, and he could see the small stones in the transparent water.

If one wanted peace, then this was where one could find it, in this place with its combination of water and trees and roses. The Le Carre which he had begun to read with its intricate doublecrossing and manoeuvring seemed very far away. All around him there was a hum of water and bees. Shadows of leaves moved across the white pages of the book and eventually he fell asleep because of the bright light and the pervasive sounds. He woke up with a start as if he had been having a terrible nightmare but he couldn't remember what it was. He looked around him in a startled way but the girl and the boy had gone and he was alone among the shadows. Through the interstices of the leaves he could see the glitter of the water. He felt cold and frightened as if some shadow had passed over him, but he could remember nothing of his dream, if dream there had been. The gravestones still leaned towards each other as if they were old men in conversation, the stream still tinkled over the stones, the bees still hummed, and once or twice a wasp planed past his face. He got up, his mouth dry, feeling suddenly that the day had turned cloudy though in fact it was still as bright as ever. He went quickly back to where Lorna was.

He found her staring at the easel which had been pitched on the ground and beside her were two of the city boys staring down at it in a blasé way, their hands hovering around their pockets. There was also a large American-looking man with a red slabby face above a hideous tie which seemed to have a combination of purple and violet in it. The two boys were grinning and saying that it had been a mistake, that they had just stumbled as they were going past. Most of the other people had turned away and were busily eating sandwiches which they had taken from picnic baskets, or were simply gazing into the water.

"Look at what these stupid gits have done," said Lorna to him when she saw him. He looked down at the picture which was wet and black with stained bootmarks. It showed beneath the dirt two large bluish mountains staring downwards into the sea as if they were studying themselves. The two boys grinned, looked at each other and then at Mark. He was still carrying the Le Carré in his hand. The American was also looking at Mark, his stomach thrust forward, as if expecting that something would happen. He was smoking a large cigar. Mark bent down to look at the painting and pick it up and as he did so he could see the legs of the two boys in their tight trousers, almost like those of cowboys.

Finally he stood up and said, "I wish you would be more careful. That's my wife's painting you've damaged."

One of the two boys who was chewing gum smiled at him and said nothing. Their shadows fell across the painting. He picked it up and handed it to Lorna who said to the two boys: "Bugger off and watch your big feet."

While she was setting up the easel again she said to Mark, "Well, you weren't much help," and then began to paint again as if nothing had happened. The two youths were aimlessly kicking at the frail wooden pier, looking over at them now and again and laughing loudly. The American with the cigar and the garish tie gazed at Mark in a puzzled way, hoisted his camera over his arm and walked slowly away.

"Did you see the way they look at you?" said Lorna. "Their eyes are like bits of glass."

"Yes, aren't they?"

"They did it just for kicks," said Lorna indignantly. "It wasn't an accident. That's why I didn't like London. Types like that."

She began to paint again and he opened his Le Carre but he couldn't concentrate. The youths were still looking towards them, talking loudly.

"Come on," he said to Lorna, "let's go down here a bit. There's a beautiful little church."

"All right," she said. "This is spoiled anyway." She got up (he carrying the easel for her) and they wandered together down to the church.

Its door was open and in the vestibule, on top of some red velvet, were some booklets, one of which he picked up, leaving a shilling as payment. There was no-one in the church but themselves. It felt cool after the heat outside. It was a very small church with the pulpit on the right hand side as they went in, facing about twenty pews cushioned with a faded red cloth. The pulpit itself was covered in a blue cloth and behind it on the wall there was a large red cross. A miniature church, it might have seated a congregation of forty or so.

They walked slowly up to the top of the church, and there they saw an effigy of a saint in bronze, lying full length on a leaden pedestal. He had calm hollow eyes and a narrow beard. His arms clutching a crozier were crossed at the breast. Above the effigy and set in the wall was an autobiography of him. Mark leaned over Lorna's shoulder to read it. It told him that the saint's name was Albertus and that he had lived in that area in the sixteenth century. Apparently he had lived by himself in the woods above the small village (which of course had not existed in its present form then) and had constituted himself the guardian of the white deer which were sometimes seen to wander among the woods, though they weren't plentiful. It was understood that they should not be hunted, for they were very rare and timid and beautiful. No-one knew where they had come from or when they had come to the area. They were considered by the local people to be symbols of good luck, and to see one was an auspicious omen. However, there had come to the estate an owner who knew little of the saint and who one day gathered a hunting party together to go out and hunt the white deer, being convinced that their flesh would be more delicate than that of the ordinary deer. He and his men were met by the saint who had argued and pleaded with them not to harm the deer. The owner of the estates, a Sir Hugh Colgon, had insisted that if the saint didn't move aside then he would put him off the lands forever. The saint had thereupon challenged him to a duel, on the result of which would depend whether the white deer would remain unmolested. So on a fine summer's day in the wood, the saint and the owner had fought a duel with swords on the green sward surrounded by the squire's (or laird's) attendants. All of them thought that the result was not in doubt, and indeed in the opening stages of the duel it seemed that the laird would win, for he was forcing the saint backwards with his huge sword which he wielded two-handed. However, just as he was about to thrust his sword home, lightning had flashed from the sky, had hovered for a moment round the laird's helmet and then flickered downwards, scorching his face in an instant so that like a tower he had fallen on the ground. His attendants of course scattered immediately and there stood the saint, sword in hand, above the dead man while from the woods around him the white deer gathered, no longer to be disturbed. The last they saw of him he was kneeling on the earth making the sign of the cross over the dead laird.

"What a beautiful story," said Lorna, gazing down into the hollow eyes which seemed to be full of light. "Do you think it really happened?"

"Unlikely," said Mark in a strange voice.

When they came out into the churchyard again they found there a small neatly-dressed man who was leaning on a stick.

"Ah," he said, tipping his hat to Lorna, "and did you enjoy the church?"

"Very much," said Lorna.

"Let me introduce myself. I'm the father of the minister in charge of the church." He spoke in a curiously measured way.

Mark had the impression that he must be about eighty years old, preserved by the good air in that protected arbour.

"I used," he added, "to be a headmaster in Garston till I retired some years ago."

Christ, another of them, thought Mark, you can't go anywhere without running across them. Even in the Garden of Eden Satan would turn out to be an academic.

"You look to me like one who would appreciate the church," the old man was saying to Lorna. "What did you think of our legend?"

"I thought it was beautiful. Is it true?"

"True? I don't know. But there are white deer around here," he said. "I've seen one once or twice."

"And do they bring good luck?"

"I don't know about that," said the old man, laughing a little. "But they certainly do exist. Actually they say that the saint was himself an ex-laird who had become religious and retired into the woods to defend the deer. That was why he even had a faint chance against the new laird who attacked him. Some people say that it was to do with an inheritance."

"Yes, they would say that, wouldn't they?" said Mark.

The old man looked at him without speaking, though for a moment it looked as if he might be about to say something.

"I don't know about their flesh though," he said, "whether their flesh is sweeter than that of ordinary deer. I did try to follow one once when I was younger but he escaped. I don't even know where they live."

"Wouldn't it be marvellous to see one," said Lorna excitedly to Mark.

"Of course."

Eventually they got away and Mark said, "I can't stand these bloody people. All these bloody dates."

"Well, he was only trying to be helpful and he is a charming man. His manners are beautiful."

"They can afford to be, living here. I wonder he isn't bored to death. Why does there always have to be someone like him around, trying to explain everything and knowing bugger all about it?"

For a moment in the church he had felt the presence of an ancient holiness, a musty smell of all the centuries that had passed since it had been built. He could imagine countless knees kneeling on the stone floor, and pale hands with hymn books. "Why do they have to corrupt everything with their dates?" he said again, "All these little bloody men among the roses."

So that they were disturbed again by the time they got into the car. In any case a fine rain was falling. Between the leaves, just as they were leaving the church, Mark saw the two youths grinning at them, their triangular heads with the small ears white between the green. When he looked again they had vanished.

"I'm sorry," he told Lorna, "he is a charming man and he probably planted all those roses himself." But Lorna didn't say anything. She appeared to be thinking of something. Suddenly he was invaded again by the shadow which had crossed him when he was asleep near the church and he put his arm around her. She looked at him briefly but didn't smile. Her yellow jersey was a little damp from the rain.

(7)

Lorna started work on a picture of the hermit. She worked at it during the afternoons when Mark was writing his thesis in another room. She did a lot of sketches of it beforehand and indeed she sometimes thought that the sketches were better than the final painting. Mark didn't know a great deal about painting though he had seen in some supplement or other drawings by some modern American painter by which he had been rather impressed.

Actually her painting of the hermit turned out to be rather like a Sutherland, a thistly being against a background of white rather like whitewash. The face was thin and whiskered, ravaged by time as if by the machinations of rats, and the whiskery lines in the face were continued or echoed in a jersey of vague stripes. After she had seen the saint's effigy in the church, part of him went into the painting also.

As she progressed with the painting she changed the background of white to one of blue so that the hermit did actually look like a thistle set against the sky. She had great difficulty with the eyes: she couldn't decide whether to make them indifferent or defiant. The hermit himself was a defiant person: he didn't really want anyone to help him and he was always complaining that she and Mrs. Carmichael were shifting his minor possessions about, including in particular a red cup with a picture of Queen Victoria on it which he had hoarded from some inconceivable past about which he would never speak a word. His room was closely crowded with all sorts of broken paraphernalia but one thing she particularly noticed was that there were no photographs. The painting of the hermit was the most difficult thing she had tried. When working at it she would completely forget about meals and smoke cigarette after cigarette. It became an obsession with her and she would become very angry with Mark if he interrupted her. She discovered much about painting from her confrontation with the hermit, possibly because he was at the opposite pole to herself, for though she had led a gipsying existence and had been at times alone her nature was to be with others.

Eventually she came to an instinctive conclusion about the eyes: they should exist as if they had forgotten about the body. The trouble was that she had no models for what she was trying to do. Tramps wouldn't do. After all, tramps moved about in society: hermits didn't. At one time she thought that perhaps she might learn something from stills of Charlie Chaplin, and for this reason would watch the extracts from silent films on the telly, but she found that these stills wouldn't do. Chaplin was gay and irreverent. She did want the hermit to be like that too, that is, she wanted to be able to make him transcend his condition, but found it difficult to do so. Her visits to him contradicted the painting she was making of him. Her visits revealed him as dirty, bad-tempered and selfish. On the other hand she was trying to make the painting rather noble.

She had him seated in the painting on an old chair with his hands clasped in front of him so tightly that they seemed to be clasping himself. At one time she would have him looking at himself in the mirror but decided that the pose would be too literary and artificial. If the hermit had been accustomed to shaving she might have got round the difficulty that way but of course he was too whiskery for that.

Even the chair presented difficulties. Would it for instance be a chair which recalled its origins in a tree? If that were accepted then the hermit would come to be accepted as part of the natural order of things, organic, necessary. On the other hand, the chair, if there was one, ought not to appear new or modern. She decided after all that she would have to eliminate the chair and make him sit on a box. She set the box upright so that he appeared precariously balanced. This gave him at one and the same time a certain appearance of hauteur combined with insecurity and a certain comicality. She made Mark sit for her in order to get the pose reasonably accurate. She didn't want any solidarity in the hermit's life. She wanted people to know immediately that he was a hermit.

As a matter of fact she had been intensely fascinated by his mode of life. She couldn't imagine how anyone could go on year after year living by himself, receiving no letters, revealing and receiving no warmth. He didn't read, he had no radio or TV. She found it almost impossible to understand how he could withstand the waves of time. She herself, she was convinced, would have gone mad, for she needed people. He must have hated the world a lot, she thought.

She spent hours trying to get his expression right. The eyes must forget the body was there at all. It was a question more of mental neglect than of physical. It was therefore not simply a question of clothes nor even of the whiskers. It was a question of making him forgetful of the world. She changed the colours a lot. She painted him in a sort of blue which seemed to fade into the blue of the sky so that he gradually seemed to recede into the world behind him. She felt, however, that by doing this she was evading the issue. She ought to try and get the expression itself right.

Eventually she got it from Mark himself. He had been reading a book and was lying back in his chair, his eyes half shut as if he had grown tired of what he was doing. His eyes took on a curiously unfocused look and staring at her he seemed not to see that she was there. She had—she could have sworn—become a part of the furniture as far as he was concerned. She got the look down on canvas immediately.

After that she had rather a lot of difficulty with the boots. On the one hand they must not appear to be too worn: they must not give the impression of having been wrinkled by travel in a real world. On the other hand they must not appear too new. They must appear as if cracked by time itself, and this disintegration must be mirrored in the face. The painting dissolved itself into a confrontation with time, for that was what being a hermit must be about. The hermit had chosen to confront time, to fight it out on its own terms, to see it eventually as a sea which he was breasting as a swimmer breasts the waves, yet at the same time becoming more unreal as he did so. She could remember noticing that unreal expression in his face as if he had lived in a different place from herself, a place without domesticities or gardens or problems. She must be able to get time into her painting, its destruction, its malignance, its vagueness. She was almost driven into a pointillist technique but decided against it.

She worked at the painting with single minded devotion. The paint itself seemed to crack under her hands so that the hermit seemed continually under the threat of disintegration by that which had actually composed him, that is the paint itself, or, transferred to another plane, time. He was being held in precarious existence by the paint which simultaneously threatened also to dissolve and leave nothing at all. She didn't realise how much of Mark's expression had gone into the painting.

She felt herself wrestling with a real problem, as real to her as her attempt to come to terms with domesticity when she had married. She had of course wanted nothing better than to be a wife but she had been frightened of what it meant, for she had not been trained for the job and again she genuinely felt that in comparison with other girls she was neither pretty nor desirable. So she grew spiritually, as she worked at the painting of the hermit. She couldn't understand what it was like to be a hermit, that life without affection, but felt at the same time that she must try to understand it, however different it was from her own.

(8)

The warm weather was merely a memory (it was December) when Lorna said to him one night, "I don't want you to go." The two of them were sitting by the double barred fire in the kitchen.

"It was me who asked," said Mark, "and I want to go."

"That's what you were talking about the night we were at the Wilkinsons', wasn't it? And you made an exhibition of yourself."

"I didn't make an exhibition of myself. I was merely pointing out the truth, that we live in a sheltered place, which is true. I want to find out what it means to see the unsheltered place."

She looked at him for a long moment, unsmilingly, and then said: "Is it impossible for you to settle down? The night we were at the Wilkinsons you went on and on about that man who was dying and who wanted to know whether the book he had written was any good or not. You offended them. Can't you see that?"

"No, I can't see that. It was a good question."

"And then you went on to talk about silent films or something stupid like that. What were you trying to show?"

"I was merely trying to show that Wilkinson, who wants a

room for showing films and doing plays, knows damn all about the cinema, or for that matter anything else."

"I see. And you do."

"Yes. I do know about silent films."

She went over to the window and looked out. The snow was gently falling, and she could see it vaguely against the darkness.

"Mark," she said without turning round, "you don't know anything about yourself, do you?"

"As much as you know about yourself perhaps. As much as anyone knows about himself."

He didn't turn round to see her standing there. "You made fun of Wilkinson with his Christmas tree and his talk about his days in Greece and Italy. You're always watching people, aren't you, studying them?"

"Not any more than anybody else."

"And that book of yours? Is it really any good?"

"I haven't finished it yet. It may be good when I finish it. It's difficult to finish it."

She spoke, still looking out of the window. "When I married you I thought you would be different from what you are. I thought of you as clever and witty. Actually you aren't like that at all, are you? I mean, you don't really know what you want. You're always on about truth and you can't see the truth about yourself. I quite like Wilkinson, and his wife if you must know. I think they are very nice people. I think they're very considerate people. And Mrs. Carmichael is the same."

"If you say so."

She came back from the window and sat on the edge of the chair. "What is it you want?" she asked.

"I am dissatisfied with what we are given," he said after a long pause. "Perhaps I am like that cousin of yours who can't stay in any school."

"And yet," she said, "you are now forty-two years old."

"Yes."

"Do you know when I met you first I thought you were very interesting. You seemed very enthusiastic. I have met more people than you have and yet I was quite struck by you even in the beginning. You seemed sure of what you were doing and that it was valuable. That is important, you know. And yet you're so unsettled now."

"All I want is to go and see these people Hunter is working among. He said he would let me know and now he has let me know. I want to go with him. Perhaps after I've done so I'll be satisfied."

"That's what you think but then after that there'll be something else. You keep on talking about that man Mrs. Carmichael and I visit. But I'd never done anything for anyone in my life. That's why I wanted to help. You don't want to help anyone. You only want to get a thrill. That's why you want to go with that friend of yours. And something could happen to you. Have you thought of that?"

"Nothing will happen to me. I'm not a child, you know. As you say yourself. I'm forty-two years old. After all, I did ask him, and it would look odd if I turned him down now."

"All right, I'll come with you then."

"No."

"Why not?"

"It's nothing to do with you. You have your hermit. You and Mrs. Carmichael. Anyway he didn't ask you. I'd prefer you not to come."

"I see."

"I don't think you see at all. I merely want to go and see for myself something everybody is talking about. It's not a terrible thing, is it? I wouldn't say it was even odd. Hunter himself works among them. People don't think that odd, do they?"

She didn't answer. He touched her cheek with his hand and she moved it away.

"What I said to Wilkinson," he said, "was perfectly right. We are privileged. I teach my literature but it doesn't mean anything any more. Can't you see that? It didn't mean anything to you."

"You don't know what you are doing," she said. "I mean

that, I don't think you know what you are doing. You touch me as if I were a toy which you forget about most of the time."

"I love you."

"I am here, that is all you can say about that." Something stirred within him for a moment and then subsided. It was like a fish rising to a hook and then moving away again.

"No," he said, "I do love you. I love to see you painting. I love to walk beside you. It's just that half the time I wonder that you should have married me. It is so strange."

"Why should it be strange? People are marrying all the time. It is not unusual."

No, it was not unusual, and yet it was strange, that two people born out of two different wombs should, after growing up, after having their experiences in the playgrounds of childhood and then in the testing places of adulthood, have come together in a particular place at a particular time. It was more than strange, it was miraculous. It was the world's most marvellous thing. Headed towards each other all those years like rockets, in ignorance of what was to come, to meet at last in the one area of the sky or earth. It was so strange it was incredible.

Suddenly he said, "I'm doing it for you."

She looked at him in amazement and then said, "I don't understand."

"I don't understand myself, but I'm doing it for you."

"You mean going there?"

"Yes."

She stood up as if she had made a decision. "Come on. Let's go and see if the snow has stopped."

They went outside and it had stopped. The sky was bright with stars which glittered feverishly.

"Let's go for a walk," she said. "Let's go out."

"It's cold," he said. "Surely you don't want to go out there now."

"Yes, I do. I do. I want to walk under the stars."

"But you would slide all over the place. It's quite slippery. And anyway where would you go?"

"Let's go to the tower and look across the harbour. It will be beautiful from there."

"No, it's too cold and anyway you would catch a cold. You've been sitting by the fire all night."

"I like the snow. We used to ski when I was in school. I remember it very well. I wasn't much good but I liked it."

As they stood in the doorway he saw the mounds of snow like clouds, like waves, and the houses weighted with it, like houses one might see on Christmas cards.

"It doesn't matter," she said, coming inside. "It just came into my head. After all, one isn't in school now. We used to wear mauve uniforms, you know." She laughed suddenly. "Imagine me in a mauve uniform."

"What happens to the birds?" she said. "Do they simply get up and go when they feel they need the warmth?"

"I suppose so."

"Just like that?" she said. "Though I don't suppose it's so odd really."

"They are said to navigate by the stars," said Mark. "At one time they couldn't make it out. Now they know they navigate by the stars."

"All right," she said, "go there tomorrow."

Her mood appeared suddenly to have changed. She kissed him suddenly and they wrestled playfully on the sofa. She pushed him away and then looked round the room.

"I was once in a hotel room at night," she said, "and I did this painting on a piece of paper resting it on the telephone directory. There was a white telephone beside me and I thought someone would ring me up but no-one did. I could have rung my father or my mother or my uncle but I didn't. I've got relations, that's one thing about me. Quite a lot really." She pulled his face towards her and then kissed him again.

"Let's go to bed," she said. In a playful mood, she said goodnight to the chair on which she was sitting, and to the chair on which Mark was sitting, and to the sofa. As he switched the light off the pale glare of the snow entered the room.

Actually the visit to the Wilkinsons had not been uninteresting. When they got there Wilkinson had been fixing a Christmas tree and seemed quite happy among the coloured bulbs. They all sat down eventually in the lounge whose walls were lined with books, most of which Mark was sure Wilkinson had never read. Mrs. Wilkinson sat in the chair knitting a shapeless blue woollen thing and it turned out that she was in fact expecting her fifth child, and this was why she was, in comparison with Lorna, so Virgin Maryish and calm and placid, only rising from her place in order to bring in sandwiches and coffee.

Lorna and Wilkinson got on very well, the latter talking about his war experiences in Greece and Italy and France and Germany.

"Actually," said his wife, "he still attends those war reunions. The other night he came back at three in the morning. He was singing one of those songs that Vera Lynn used to sing. I hope the neighbours didn't hear."

"I'm sure they didn't," said Wilkinson. "As a matter of fact I was watching TV the other night and they were showing this War reunion which Mountbatten had with his Burma troops. Vera Lynn was singing and there were two sisters there also doing an act. I thought they looked very old. It made me realise how old I was getting myself."

"Fifty," said his wife smiling.

"For people like us of course," said Wilkinson with his usual enthusiasm, "the war was the only means we had of seeing the world though I suppose it's a terrible thing to say. I once saw the Acropolis by moonlight. There's a man, I think his name is Bowler, who wrote a book about Greece which I read. I don't know if you know him, Mark. He also wrote a book about South America. It's called *Days in the Saddle*."

The finest of *The Readers' Digest*, said Mark under his breath. "No," he said aloud, "I haven't read it."

"I think you've done quite a bit of travelling yourself," said Wilkinson to Lorna who had been watching Mrs. Wilkinson knitting.

"Yes, yes I have. Not that I learned much. People like me never notice anything."

"Oh I wouldn't say that," said Mark. "I think she writes the most interesting letters. She notices a lot."

"The places get all jumbled up in one's mind," said Lorna. "Lots of people travel and notice nothing."

"That's quite true," said Wilkinson. "I visited Italy myself. I didn't like the people much. I much preferred the Greeks. I didn't like the Egyptians either."

"The loneliest I ever felt in my life was in South Africa," said Lorna. "All these veldts or whatever they call them. The sky goes on forever. I had the most intense feeling that I wanted to be with people. I'm afraid I can't stand much loneliness. That's why I like it here. The people are very nice and friendly."

"Quite," said Mark. "Mind you, small towns have their drawbacks."

"Naturally," said Wilkinson. "One doesn't see much of the world."

"I wasn't thinking of that so much," said Mark. "I was thinking of the local newspaper. I mean, everything is so good. The whist drive, the prize giving, the local concert, they're all good. And yet when one actually goes they're stupendous bores."

"Well," said Wilkinson, "people don't want to be unpleasant, do they?"

"I suppose so." Mark leaned forward in his chair and said: "There is one thing I meant to ask you all in connection with that. Some time ago a man whom I was friendly with died. Before he died he'd been writing a novel, and he had never done any writing before in his life. You know the kind of person? He thinks that writing is something anyone can do, and during his working life he despises it. After all, everyone uses words. He would never dream of trying to write a symphony. In any case, this man was dying and he knew he was dying. He also knew of course that I read rather a lot. So one night he brought out this sheaf of paper and said to me: 'Would you care to read what I've been writing? Naturally it isn't as good as what you normally read.' I took the sheaf of papers and there was the kind of embarrassed silence you get in situations like that. I didn't take long to realise that the novel was sheer rubbish, the kind of thing you might get from a schoolboy of fifteen. So I was in rather a difficult situation. There was no doubt that the man knew he was dying. There was also no doubt that he wanted me to say that the book was a good one." He stopped and looked around him. "Well, what should I have said?"

"That is a pretty problem," said Wilkinson. "I myself taking everything into account would have said that it was a good book, whether I believed it or not. I had rather an interesting case when I was in Greece. I had suspicions that this private's wife was deceiving him. You know that in those days we censored all the letters? In any case, one day this letter came to him and I had a strong suspicion that she was telling him that she was leaving him. So I held the letter back. Actually we were going over the top the following day. When I read the letter it confirmed what I had thought. You remember, Norma," he said to his wife, "I told you about it? In any case, the private was killed in action. Technically perhaps I had done something wrong but how could you expect a man to go into action knowing that his wife had left him?"

"You didn't give him the chance of knowing the truth?" said Mark.

"No, and I believe I did right. I think there are certain things we ought not to know, even about ourselves. He would have got to know about it eventually but I didn't want him to face a battle with that on his mind."

"I think you were quite right dear," said his wife, knitting placidly. "I don't see what else you could have done."

"And what about you, Mrs. Simmons," said Wilkinson, while Mark was thinking that it was typical of him that he should have reduced the substance of his question to a triviality.

"I don't know," said Lorna slowly. "It's difficult. On the one hand, I suppose artistic standards must be kept high. On the other hand, perhaps a human being is more important than a work of art. That is really what you are saying, isn't it, Mark." She was thinking that Mark seemed incapable of small talk, that he was always getting people involved in argument. Through the open door of the lounge she could see the Christmas tree with its coloured bulbs and felt more at home than she did in her own house. Mark hated Christmas trees.

"I suppose it is," said Mark. "I suppose what I'm really saying is that in small towns the truth is hidden away in the attic, that no-one will admit to what he is. I remember I had an argument rather like this once with some visitors who were taking Bed and Breakfast in my lodgings and they took it very badly. They were English people. As a matter of fact it emerged that one of them was a physicist, quite a clever man in his own field but, I should imagine, rather stupid outside it."

"What would you have liked yourself?" said Wilkinson, pouring some whisky into glasses. "Would you have liked to be told?"

"I think so," said Mark. "Yes, I think so."

There was a silence and then Mrs. Wilkinson got up and said, "After that I think we should have some tea." Lorna was looking at Mark in a rather grim way, as if she hoped that he would move on to something less explosive, but he did not seem to be thinking about her. His face was pale and intent and, she thought, rather thin. Why couldn't he be like Wilkinson, she wondered. Why couldn't he be relaxed, spending an evening working at a Christmas tree? But no, that seemed to be impossible for him. He was always confronting these insoluble questions, a man out in a white storm.

"I find that golf cures me of asking these kinds of questions," said Wilkinson, "The wind on your face, you know. There's nothing better to give you a sense of proportion."

Mark turned away and began to examine the titles of the

books on the shelves. He always crosses his knees, thought Lorna, and he always looks very tense.

"As a matter of fact," said Mark, "there's a friend of mine in Glasgow who does some work with juvenile delinquents. I'm going to see him fairly soon."

"Oh, isn't that dangerous?" said Mrs. Wilkinson who had just come in. "They attack people with knives, don't they?"

"Not always," said Mark shortly.

Lorna was furious. She had been told nothing about this by Mark and if she had been at home she would have started a quarrel. But she didn't say anything at that time.

"I think," said Wilkinson, passing the tea, "we are very lucky to be where we are. One or two?" he said to Lorna.

"Two, please, or even three."

"None for me, thanks," said Mark. "I don't take sugar." He was thinking how much prettier Lorna was than Mrs. Wilkinson. Don't let her ever grow like Mrs. Wilkinson, he muttered under his breath. Don't let her ever become plump and nice and happy and relaxed. Let her always retain that curious Red Indian look of hers. Let her never learn to play bingo. But he knew that she would be trapped like everybody else. He knew that she wasn't as strong in loneliness as he was. As he thought of her becoming like Mrs. Wilkinson he felt a pain that pierced him deep in the heart, a pain such as he had never felt in his life before. To think of her sitting in a chair knitting woollens, or at a table in a restaurant wearing a pale bracelet over a brown jumper of fine wool, made him ache with fear. Oh God, he thought, let her be more vital than that, let her rather dabble with her paints forever in dirty denims.

Lorna was now talking to Wilkinson about her painting. Her face glowed and she became wholly alive.

"Of course he wouldn't sit for me," she said, "he sits by himself in that dirty room. I have to try and remember what he looks like. I have to get the exact unshaven look into his face."

"There's a painting by Van Gogh a little like that," said Wilkinson. "He was the man who cut off his ear or somebody else's ear, I can never remember," he said to his wife. "He looked very unshaven in that painting. And then of course there's Gauguin. He was the one who went off to the South Seas. Just like Robert Louis Stevenson."

They talked about painting for a while and then got on to the silent film, a subject which was introduced rather maliciously by Mark in order to find out how much Wilkinson knew.

"I remember seeing them a long time ago," he said. "I remember matinees. Of course we were very poor in those days. I always associate them with poverty."

"You could learn a lot from the silent films for your painting," said Mark to Lorna. "You want a more imagistic technique. Her paintings are rather moral," he told the Wilkinsons.

When they had had their tea, Wilkinson discoursed at great length on the Christmas tree, where and when he had bought it and how much it had cost. It turned out that he was later going to donate it to a Children's Hospital. He also spent a long time discussing the incidence of burst pipes in cold weather.

Around eleven o'clock Mark and Lorna got up. She had clearly enjoyed her evening. She was in good spirits and her colour was good.

"When are you expecting the child?" she asked Mrs. Wilkinson.

"About a month or so. Last time my husband was in a terrible state, ringing the hospital at all hours of the night. Mind you, they're very nice here. You can go and visit any time you like, practically."

When Lorna and Mark were walking down the road they passed the lakes where the two swans had been. It was now frozen over.

"I wonder if swans migrate," said Mark. "I suppose they do. Even Leda's swan," and he burst out laughing.

Lorna's face looked very pale in the reflected snow and starlight.

"You didn't tell me about that friend of yours," she said.

"Oh, the one who deals with the delinquents? I'm sorry, I

forgot. You should meet him, he's very interesting and he writes damn good books."

"To hell with his books," said Lorna suddenly. "To hell with him and his books."

"What are you so angry about now?"

"Well you want people to tell you the truth, don't you? That's how I feel, that's all. And I'm telling you."

"All right, all right, so you're telling me. Let's leave it at that, shall we?"

"No, we won't leave it at that. Did you notice how warm that house was? Our house always seems to be so cold."

"They've got better heating. Wilkinson gets up and stokes it in the morning before he goes to college."

"Oh, shut up."

"You shut up," he said, putting his arms around her. Her face enclosed by the furs was diamond like and clear, like a pearl of dew.

"My beautiful Lorna," he said, "what is Mrs. Wilkinson to you? She is three thousand feet below you. She is on the plains and you are on the mountains. She is a bloody swamp devouring old Wilkinson. You are worth three million of her. Three bloody million."

"I'm not so sure," said Lorna in a small quiet voice. "I'm not so sure."

(10)

When he got on the train (having bought a *Statesman* at the bookstall to read on the way) there was no-one in the carriage but himself and a coloured man who had a case beside him, as if he had been selling clothes. The carriage contained a large number of seats of soft cushiony green stuff and tables and Mark sat down in a corner seat near the door. Outside, it was cold and the roads were slippery: he could imagine that not many people would wish to come out. However, there was no snow falling and the air was dry.

He began to read the *Statesman* and to think about his coming adventure with a certain excitement. He wasn't quite clear in his mind about what world Hunter might show him, but he expected that it would be at least interesting and unusual. He wasn't frightened in any way, merely curious, for though he had read much about violence he had never come into contact with anyone who had committed it. In fact he expected that the people he might see would be quite pleasant to him: after all, he himself was an egalitarian and he had no preconceptions against them.

From his corner seat he could see the head of the coloured man leaning back against the green cushiony seat as if he were tired. The bulging case beside him was strapped tightly as if he hadn't succeeded in selling much. He wondered idly how coloured men reacted to the bitter cold December and why they remained in such a cold country when they could go back to their own. Did they expect more than they got when they came and then refuse out of stubbornness to return? Presumably they were tired and dispirited walking street after street with their cases, being greeted contemptuously by people from an alien culture. He wondered how he would feel himself if he went to India or Pakistan, a stranger, to walk from village to village, house to house, selling goods which perhaps nobody really wanted. Sitting in the carriage he had an immense intuition of loneliness, of the loneliness of the black man in front of him, of a life lived in utter loneliness, when one had in common with other people neither a language nor a culture nor even a gesture. As the train hummed on he turned this idea over and over in his mind, as a jeweller might examine a stone, looking at it from all angles in the slant, slightly flawed air. It would be as if one were at a certain angle to the universe, hanging upside down in a world without gravity.

As he studied the head (he couldn't see the face) he noticed that the hair was turning slightly grey. He had never noticed a greying coloured man before, or rather the greying head of a coloured man. It was leaning back against the green stuff as if the man were tired, as if he did not even know that there was any observer in the carriage, as if, even if there were, he didn't care. He didn't turn his head at all, not even to look out of the window to see if there was any interesting scenery or to study the names of the stations. Perhaps he had sold nothing all that day: this might even be his form of communication, and to sell nothing would be a criticism of himself. Perhaps selling something involved a kind of love which he was missing, and, missing that, he had nothing.

Mark was amazed and made uneasy by the thoughts that the head of the coloured man brought into his mind. Perhaps if he could see his face the thoughts would go away and he might even see a jolly happy face unwrinkled by the cares of the day. After all, coloured people were often joyful and vivacious: one had only to think of people like Louis Armstrong, holding the trumpet to their mouths. But this was probably not a Negro: he would be an Indian or a Pakistani, and no-one knew what they were like; at least he didn't.

As he was thinking these thoughts, the sliding doors at one end of the carriage slid open and two tall youths strode through, shouting loudly. They walked quickly down the corridor and opened the door next to him and went into the next carriage. He had a quick glimpse of skin-tight blue trousers and belts and then they were gone, leaving the door beside him open. The draught began to blow against his shoulder and he sat up and pulled the door shut again. He tried to go back to his *New Statesman*, where he was reading an article on economics.

In a short while the door behind him opened again and the two youths strode, singing and shouting, down the corridor again. This time they stopped just before they reached the door at the far end and looked back. As they did so he looked down quickly at his *Statesman*. He felt suddenly chilled as if there had entered the carriage a strange scent of the beast of prey, a vulpine air, as if he himself were crouching down behind the *Statesman* like a small creature in the undergrowth, hoping not to be noticed, but scenting the rank smell of death all around it.

They were however not looking at him: they were looking

at the coloured man. In unison, like a caricature of dancers, they wafted towards him and stood looking down at him, impersonal as neon light, or warped scientists examining something on a slide. One of them lovingly touched the top of his head. The black head did not stir but presumably the face stared ahead of it, without winking, an object which knew its place, or which had learned that to give offence by moving was to attract the lightning. One of the youths delicately stroked the head as one might stroke the head of a dog, lovingly, carefully, as if the youth had found something of unexpected value which he must not lose. They looked at each other. Mark looked at them askance.

"Coon," said one of the youths in a wondering voice, "a coon. A nice wee coon." The other one smiled angelically, his fair hair framing a cherubic face. "A coon," he repeated. Still the head remained motionless, and the mouth speechless. The first youth patted the head possessively, and they walked on towards the door and through it. There was a silence in the carriage: the black head all this time hadn't moved. But the silence in the carriage was the silence before thunder, the silence of a heavy day with a coppery sky when one waits for something to happen. Mark felt a constriction at his heart. He felt as if he were being slowly squeezed to death. He thought: I will get up and I will go and sit beside the coloured man. I shall sit there beside him and then they will have to attack me as well. But he sat where he was. The train sped on.

The door opened and the two youths came back. One of them (the one with the fair hair and the cherubic face) stood above the coloured man and said gently, but loudly enough for Mark to hear, "We're going to do you, coon." His voice was infinitely gentle, infinitely patient. He might have been a doctor reassuring a patient that there was nothing wrong, he might have been a lover whispering to his loved one. "When you get off at the station we're going to do you, coon." Mark could see no black face, only a head that didn't move, and the head was a target in the middle of concentric groves that receded and advanced, receded and advanced. It was strange that the head didn't move at all, not even towards the youths. It was as if it expected these things to happen to it continually as stones expect the rain. It leaned there against the green, the face staring straight ahead.

"Where do you come from, coon?" said the youth leaning towards the face. "When did you wash yourself last, coon? When did you, coon? Don't you like me, coon? Say something, coon?" He put his arm around him as if he were cradling a child. The train sped on, making little sound, neither jerking to the right nor to the left. "Tell you what, coon, we'll be behind you when you get off at the station. There's a lavatory there. That's where we'll do you, coon. Do you get me, coon?" The face was infinitely gentle, the voice was infinitely patient. Mark was almost lulled to sleep by it, till he tried to imagine what the face of the coloured man looked like, till he tried to imagine what he must feel, till he tried to imagine the coloured man thinking of the lavatory at the station, the darkness of it, the scrawled obscenities, the large tiled whitenesses.

He looked out of the window. They sped through another station and no-one boarded the train. He could imagine most people sitting by the fire, by their Christmas trees, preparing for their festivities, drawing in from the outer cold. At one station a man with a wheelbarrow waved to them and one of the youths waved back, out of his largesse, his satisfied leisure. He had pleasure ahead of him, the world was pleasant and opulent.

The three people in front of him had fallen silent, waiting there as in a frieze, the black man sitting, the fair haired youth half-sitting beside him, and the other one standing, looking down. A trinity. An obscene trinity. A companionship which was very close, so close that they could sense each other's blood ticking. The train hummed on.

If I were to pull the communication cord, thought Mark, then surely someone would come. He looked at it, and, as he looked, one of the youths looked back at him and smiled but made no move towards him. He dropped his eyes. He stared at the *Statesman* but he didn't read anything. The youth came along and looked down at him. "It's a coon," he said. "Do you know what a coon is?" There was a long silence. "It's a coloured man, isn't it?" he heard himself saying. The youth seemed satisfied. "You're right," he said, "dead on. Dead on." He moved back down to where the coloured man was. The train sped on, accelerating. It seemed to be stopping at fewer stations now. He clenched his hands thinking, "I hope we don't pass through any tunnels. I hope we don't pass through any tunnels." He imagined the blackness and he was frightened. He was terrified. His hands sweated, his spirit sweated. But it was broad daylight all the time and the fair-haired youth seemed to be crooning to the coloured man, seemed to be singing a lullaby to him, his most precious possession, his own, his child. And the black head did not move. It waited. It perhaps thought but it did not speak. It was greying.

It will go on like this forever, thought Mark, forever and forever. If only the man would say something, if only he would protest. If only he would shift his head. If only he would look at the two youths. But the train hummed on, picking up speed, rocking from side to side. But it did not shake that head. It was set in the gap between two wedges of cushiony green. It was fixed. And then the terrifying feeling swam into Mark's mind: perhaps there is only the head. Perhaps there is no body. Perhaps there is no suit, no tie, no trousers, no shoes, just the head that has been suffering and fixed since time began. The two youths were almost asleep, bringing home their coloured head like a trophy that a hunter might bring home after a long day in the woods with his gun, searching, and then by pure chance, by radiant opportunity, coming across in a clearing a gift as if from the heavens themselves, a victim, a deer.

The train approached the station, decelerating, passing large wooden warehouses, negotiating a spider's web of rails, shining, icy. The platform sped towards them. There was a long release of air as if somebody had sighed, and the train stopped.

"Come on then, coon," said one of the youths. "Don't

forget your case." There was a long silence. No doors seemed to be opening, and there was hardly anyone on the platform. One of them took his case, and they got him up out of his seat. Mark noticed the scuffy shoes, one heel lower than the other, and the brown baggy trousers, with a patch at the back. He saw the short squat baggy figure moving forward between the two youths who were supporting him as if he were a drunk or a sick man whom they were helping along. He heard a loud thin silent scream coming from inside himself as he watched the three walking along. The scream was like cloth being ripped. He touched his lips as if he felt that blood was coming from them. Behind him the steam sighed and hissed, freezing as it touched the air. He half stumbled out past the ticket collector into the square, standing there for a moment staring unseeingly at the statue of Kitchener and the stone lions below the suspended yellow sword.

In front of him he saw a pub and entered, ordering a whisky quickly. He drank it in one gulp and ordered another one. In a short while he would go to Hunter's house and they would go to wherever Hunter was taking him. He stared at a girl perched on a bar stool, her short skirt hitched about her thighs. She stared back at him angrily and he swivelled his eyes away. A Negro was sitting on one of the stools with his arm around one of the barmaids, telling her a joke in a loud voice. Then he burst out laughing, hands slapping his knees, an animated child. The middle aged barman said, "Sexy bugger, aren't you?" The Negro laughed again and said something to his friend who was reading a newspaper. They both laughed.

Mark got up and went out into the cold day. He felt strange, almost lightheaded, as if some bubble were rising in his head, as if the world itself had been transformed into a bubble, transparent, slightly odd, drifting.

He made his way in the direction of Hunter's house, which he hadn't visited before. He asked directions from a number of people who didn't seem very clear about where it was. Eventually he came to the close and stood staring up at it, thinking. The white stairs faced him, looking empty and clean.

A drunk man wove past singing. The harsh wintry light rebounded from the stones: ahead of him he saw a large glassy structure. He waited. Then his feet started to move, away from the close. He didn't want to see Hunter after all. He walked unsteadily along till he came to a cinema which was showing a Scandinavian film. He climbed the plushy stairs to the circle and sat down in the expensive seats at the back. The large figures on the screen swam towards him, moonily. They were dancing in the twilight by a white expanse of lake, and the air seemed full of symbolism. They had large naked lunar buttocks rounded as the luminous tent in the background. He couldn't concentrate on them at all, he couldn't imagine what the story (if story there was) was about. The fragments of conversation seemed ridiculously trite though apparently intended to be profound. Soon there were two of them lying down in a birch wood in the variegated moonlight and another two were diving into the water. Lips approached each other, hands fumbled at flesh.

He thought of something Hunter had said and the words swam into his mind as if they formed a subtitle to a foreign film.

"They are incapable of affection." The words beat inside his head drumlike. "They are incapable of affection. They don't like to be touched." And then Lorna saying, "What do the birds do? Do they just take off?" As if in a film he saw fragmentary pictures, himself saying, "Intellectual honesty is everything." The lovers swarmed about each other. "You're a spiritual tourist." He saw himself bending down towards the picture in that small village and the legs of the two youths, stiff and tall above him. He saw himself working at his thesis and above the thesis he saw the picture of the hermit, unshaven and taut faced. He left the circle and went downstairs to the lavatory. His face looked white and shocked as if prised out of wrinkled cement.

"Oh my God," he thought, "she's left me." And he knew quite clearly that she had left him, he knew that her dance the night before had been a farewell to the house. He knew that

he had destroyed himself. As he went outside, the neon lighting seemed to be flashing out quotations, a script for his life, his
literary life, "Have you ever been alone, truly alone?" someone seemed to be saying. "Have you ever been truly, really,
alone?" He seemed to be suddenly at odds with the universe.
When was the next train back? He rushed now to the station.
Another hour. He waited in the waiting room.

As he waited, more and more pictures cut into his mind
and hung there straight in front of him. A voice seemed to be
saying to him, "You are a mediocrity. You didn't know anything about yourself. You didn't know reality. You thought it
was like literature." He thought of Wilkinson and his wife
ensconced in their warm room with the Christmas tree. He
thought of him entrenched behind the battlements of the
possible.

"They are incapable of affection." The words came at him
like knives out of the greying air. "They don't like to be
touched. They are fighting not you, you are just an excuse,
you have got in their way." He stumbled into the lavatory.
There was blood on the floor and he stared at it as if at something which he ought to remember about, something he ought
to know the origin of. But there was no-one at all in the lavatory. If only the black man were still there. But there was
no-one. He saw the scribblings on the wall and recognised
them not as the script from an exciting world but as the in-
fantile fantasia of the impotent. He could himself write
something there, "We are incapable of affection." He could
write it in blood, his own blood.

"Oh my God," he said to himself, "what have you done?
What have you done?" A quotation came into his mind, "richer
than all its tribe." He stared down at his shoes trying to think
of what went before that. "A pearl." Something about a pearl.
Let me see her again in all the tea rooms in existence with the
pearls around her throat, he thought. But he knew he wouldn't
see her again. Tears pricked his eyes, and he put his handkerchief to them, behind the glasses.

"Have you ever been lonely, really lonely? I love this place."

He put his hand to his cheeks. They seemed unshaven, untidy. His shoes looked unpolished. But then he had never been really tidy. That was part of his persona. That was part of the mask.

Absentmindedly the point of his shoe moved among the thin blood, writing "They are incapable of affection. They are incapable of affection." He left the lavatory and went back to the waiting room where a woman was wiping the nose of a small girl and saying something to her fiercely. The girl kicked at the shopping basket and the woman said, "Wait till I get you home. You wait, my girl." He looked at them with intolerable longing as if at angels in a heaven he would never enter. The world had been too strange for him, too miraculous. The ordinary had been too miraculous. It had given too much but he could not see it. The train stood at the platform with its lighted carriages, houses of the ordinary day.

(11)

As he expected, he found the house empty and its emptiness was of a kind such as he had never experienced before. The only image that pricked itself on his mind like a thorny tattoo was an abandoned space ship and himself floating through space holding on to such reality as there was by a life line so thin that it could hardly be seen against the sky. The post had been since Lorna had left and he stared dully down at some Christmas cards which were lying on the floor of the lobby.

From the wardrobe her clothes were gone: in his own wardrobe the clothes remained. He wandered from room to room not thinking, just existing and throbbing, and in the kitchen came face to face with the picture of the hermit which she had been working on. Shivering uncontrollably he turned its face to the wall and sat down, automatically switching on the fire, the switch for which he could reach from the chair. Raising his eyes to the mantelpiece he saw the envelope with his name on it. He stared at it for a long time not daring to open it, it seemed so final. He remembered sometimes how she would write messages on the backs of cheques in her quick round scrawl. She had gone away in the gipsyish way she had come, carelessly, without regard for her possessions except her clothes, casting herself on the world again. Even the painting she had left behind: she didn't depend on him.

Eventually he opened the envelope. The familiar round scrawl met his eyes. There was no Dear Mark, the letter went straight into its subject matter.

"When you come back I shall have left. It never has worked and it never will work. You are not a real person. I think that's what it is. You aren't real. You said you disliked Wilkinson but he at least is real. It's not just that you are always talking about books and the thesis you'll write, it's just that you aren't real. I could never even touch you and you could never touch me. I can't think of any other way of describing you. Other people live like you and yet they are real. At one time, when I saw you first, you were witty and interesting. But I think that was an illusion (or should that be delusion?). I am unhappy going away but not for leaving you. I liked the place. I said the other night that I had relatives and I know you haven't any. I am worried by that but I know you won't do anything silly.

[Anything heroic, she means, he thought, the bile rising in his mouth. Anything real.]

I did try, you know. I am a clumsy person but I did try. I wasn't afraid at least to try. I wasn't afraid of being un-dignified. I don't think I was afraid of failing. The thing was you never thought about me at all. I could have stood anything except the unreality. I thought I was a child: people were always saying that I was a child. But I think I'm a different child from you. I shall be all right. The last straw was your going away today just to see these people.

It showed me once and for all that you would never grow up, that you want to go to the pictures all the time. There's no point in looking for me. I shan't come back."

On the mantelpiece beside the letter was the ring he had given her. He picked it up and absentmindedly tried to fit it on to his finger but it wouldn't fit. Then he thought that if it rolled from the mantelpiece it would be lost so he put it inside an aspirin bottle from which he emptied out all the aspirins. From the cupboard he took the half bottle of whisky which had been bought for Christmas and began to drink it steadily, thinking as he did so of the night he had gone to her house. That was bravado, this was reality.

He drank steadily and much later he could recall Mrs. Carmichael and Wilkinson being in the house and talking in hushed voices and Mrs. Carmichael saying (he could hear her for his hearing had grown preternaturally sharp): "You see, when Lorna came here she was terrified. She had been wandering about all her days. She had never been given any affection by anyone. She wanted to settle down here and she didn't want to move. She wouldn't even go to the city to look at the pictures in the Art Gallery. She was very insecure you know. I think that was why she wanted to help with the hermit, because she knew about loneliness." Her voice came to him through a drunken haze, the vowels and consonants seemed to shift and change.

"How is he?" he heard her saying some time later. That was her speaking to her doctor husband, he thought, and then he saw the doctor's violet coloured burnt face floating around him, an improbable phantasm.

"Physically he's all right. Just the shock."

"What are you going to do about him?"

"He should take some sleeping pills, and go to bed. You can come and make his breakfast in the morning."

"I can do that."

Later he heard her moving about the house, fixing the bed, and then later still he heard the voice of Wilkinson.

"How is he? Terrible thing. I came over as soon as you phoned."

"He's a bit shocked. In fact badly shocked."

Mark stretched his hand out for the whisky bottle and it crashed to the hearth. He heard it breaking without distress or joy: it was simply another event in a universe of pain.

"He could come and stay with us tonight," said Wilkinson. "We would be happy to have him. If we could get something together. Shaving gear and things like that."

He found himself, without knowing much about it, in Wilkinson's car, Wilkinson not speaking at all, as they drove along, and Mark's head lolling against the leather coverings of the back seat. He was thinking, There's always a Horatio around, isn't there, someone who will pick up the pieces after a sordid little affair which doesn't even deserve being called a tragedy. And then he thought: Lorna wouldn't like these quotations. Lorna wouldn't like this being converted into literature. Will I never stop, he agonised, will I never stop setting this grid over reality?

But that wasn't what was wrong after all. It was something else. It was mediocrity, that was what it was.

"Up we get," said Wilkinson heaving him out of the door and taking him into the house. There were flashes of lights and then he was lying in a clean white bed in pyjamas that were too large for him (something about that in *Macbeth*, ticked the lights from his mind which never rested). He shut his eyes.

"I did not know that she was afraid too," he thought. "I thought it was she who was the aristocrat and I who was the frightened one."

He remembered vaguely how Wilkinson had undressed him, some whispered words to his wife (she seemed to be saying in answer, "He never liked you, you know") and then he was being carried into the bedroom like a child.

They would be talking about him, they would be arranging his future for him, they would already be reading the documents. They knew about things like that, they were more solid than he was, his irony was comic. All that time Wilkinson had been capable of all this, the ease of action, of putting pyjamas on him, of carrying him to that bed. That was part of the moving world for him, he didn't need to think about it.

He wondered what colour the pyjamas were.

"Court jester," he thought. "Comedian."

And I did it all for her, he thought. For Lorna. I wanted to find out. I wanted to become real, because I knew I was less than real. And all the time we were at cross purposes.

He felt her presence suddenly in the room, definably, like a perfume, and sat up in bed, but of course there was no-one there.

Horror stricken he stared into the darkness. It was as if ahead of him he could see himself disintegrating and in his place the picture of the hermit or the face of Wilkinson, one frowning, the other genially smiling, holding out a welcoming hand.

And also he saw Lorna setting her face into the shifting world again, the cheques with their messages drifting around her like snowflakes, and being met by two youths who were whispering into her ear, tenderly close to the black hair;

"What a lovely coon you are, what a lovely coon."

So distinct was the picture that he must have shouted out from the world of bed and wardrobe and bookshelf and table and chair for Wilkinson came to the door, switched on the light and said in his easy voice:

"It's all right. You're with us. You're quite safe. Shall I leave the light on?"

"No," he said without thinking, then quickly, "Yes, please leave it on."

Part three

He stood at the window of the hotel watching the whirling snow, its drifting intricate leisurely dance. He had given up thinking. Images floated about in his mind but he wasn't thinking. Strangely enough, one of them was from long ago, the discussion about *Hamlet* in the cafe and the little waitress in the white uniform with the red at the breast. He felt that there was something there that he ought to understand because it was somehow important. All around him the pipes of the hotel wheezed, like someone with lung trouble.

The trouble was of course that he had nowhere to go. He had come by a blind route to an end. In mathematics if one came to a problem that one couldn't work out one abandoned it: in life one simply endured it. In mathematics you leave it, in life you live it, he rhymed mercilessly to himself.

He thought of Frith who had come home to a fireplace after the abyss. But he himself could never do that. Once in the abyss one was coloured by its light forever and forever. Perhaps even Frith was, and his rubicund appearance was merely a mask such as one might wear at a Christmas party or at Hallowe'en. Perhaps below the smart doll-like clothes there was a city raped and torn by mental wars, by an alien occupation.

If this were a book, he thought, there would be a rational ending. At least there would have been in Victorian times. The author would tell what had happened to all the characters, how Jill had married Tom, how everyone had got what he or she deserved, how the world after all was inhabited by an artistic justice. But in the twentieth century this was no longer possible. In this world there were jagged flashes of unfinished anecdotes, theses and antitheses, edgings of lightning.

"But at least," he said to himself, "you know about yourself now. And that is something. You have been stripped to the bare bone. You know your assets." And he began, as a business man might, to add up these assets. "You are five foot ten, you wear glasses, you weigh 110 pounds, you have a sufficiency of clothes. You have a mind that is irretrievably romantic in a world that is no longer so, but believes no longer in the hero. The hero is no longer the man on the frontier of things, he goes into space but describes the earth seen from the moon in the language of a bank manager."

The snow swirled and swirled. Perhaps he should go in search of Lorna, that would be his pilgrimage. He would find her after many years and he would say, "I was wrong. I will do anything you wish. I will be whatever you wish me to be. I will no longer be the mental aristocrat, the aloof ridiculous backward man." Homo textual.

But as he looked into the varying patterns of the snow he knew that he had come to the end of a certain road, that he had forced himself by some inner compulsion to the limits, that after all this was where he must have wanted to be, in the coldness of truth. Everyone got what they deserved in a way the Victorian novelists did not dream of.

Ahead of him he saw an advertisement for something or other that he could not make out because of the snow flashing on and off in red. It entered him, and he let it enter him. Everything could enter him. He was a mirror open to the doings of the universe. He was as open as a door. Anything, anybody could walk through and take up its place in him. Even the future. Whatever that meant.